FANTASTIC FABLES OF FOSTER FLAT

FLAT

BOOK #2

ORRIN JASON BRADFORD

I0534238

You may also enjoy the science fiction technothriller FreeForm series.
Pick up your free copy of Crash, the prequel at:

www.wbradfordswift.com/crashlanding[1]

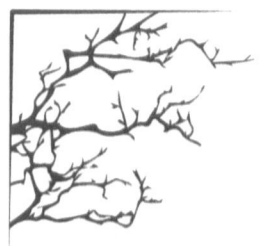

Introduction

I thought I'd shared all the strange happenings of my birthplace, Foster Flat, in the first book. Then, one night, when I was feeling particularly lonely sitting in my cubby-hole of an apartment here in Atlanta, I pulled out several of the journals I've kept through the years. What I found shocked me. I spent all that night and much of the next day circling passages and inserting post-its at the start of each strange tale. Thus began the book that you now hold in your hands. Over the next few weeks, I sorted through the journals in search of the stories that I felt most represented the unique nature of my hometown.

It's likely, if you've read the first anthology, you'll recognize a few of the Foster Flat citizens, though most will be new to you. For sure you should remember my dear Aunt Ellenore. You know, the one who found her muse sitting on her front porch. But muses are a bit like a set of keys. You find them, then lose them, then find them again. At least in Ellenore's case, she became wiser for the experience.

Then there's Albert Goldman, who owns Goldcraft, Inc., one of the coolest stores in town, with the oddest assortment of nicknacks displayed in the front window. Especially when you consider it's mostly a jewelry and watch repair business. A couple of my classmates swore to me it was also the location of a most bizarre, yet true, story. Now, there were quite a few kids I went to school with that I would never trust to tell the truth, but Randall and Pee Wee were not among them. They were straight shooters.

Just like Reginald and Daisy Davis—two upstanding citizens of Foster Flat who took their love for travel and exotic masks and turned them into a business known simply as the Mask Museum. I visited the museum quite often, but never at night, even though Daisy invited me to come by any time. It was just too spooky for any late night excursions. Daisy maintained the museum for years after her husband passed on to the everlasting, though she claimed to be just as close to him as though he were still alive.

There's also a story about one of my favorite eating establishments—Lin Shu's Chinese Pagoda Restaurant. They serve some of the best Asian food anywhere. I've yet to find a place here in Atlanta that compares. While I didn't know Wilbur that well since he worked at the Pagoda only one summer, he swore that every bit of his story was true, and I have no reason to doubt him. After all, his uncle, Mr. Alfred Peterman, is one of the deacons at the Baptist church my family attends. I feel certain Wilbur knows it's a sin to lie, especially to a future journalist.

While Lin Shu's is a wonderful place to go for lunch or dinner, you simply can't beat the Apothecary for a good ol' southern breakfast. I don't know how Fatima does it, maintaining the restaurant in the front of the store while running her natural healing practice in the back rooms, but she does, despite a few challenges she had with the North Carolina Medical Board of Examiners a while back.

Of course, not all parts of Foster Flat are as upstanding as our Main Street downtown area. You might recall a story about the strange happenings around the Seventh Avenue district. Well, not far from there, another story unfolded one cold Christmas season. When I heard the tale, I was honored to be a part of such a fine community with such wonderful people as Emily Lawson. My word, but that woman is a saint, even if she is a Methodist. She's still good Christian folk.

Now, at first I wasn't going to include the two last stories, but then I remembered that my job as a journalist is to report the facts as best I know them. True, little Jimmy Brown may not be the most reliable source I ever interviewed, though since working at *The Global Inquiry,* I've spoken with several less reliable witnesses (and their stories made it into the paper). As for the last story...well, I'm the primary source for that one so I know it's the truth, the whole truth, and nothing but the truth, so help me God.

Mimi Rawlins
Roving Reporter for *The Global Inquiry*
Born and raised in Foster Flat, North Carolina

ELLENORE LOSES HER MUSE

Ellenore Michner held the phone away from her ear to lessen the audio assault from her agent, Rachel Mohaney, blasting through the line. The words were still clear as a bell. "I can't put the publisher off much longer. They've been more than patient, but they have a schedule they need to maintain."

Ellenore waited for the inevitable pause for Rachel to catch her breath before replying, "No worry. It's almost finished, really it is. I'm just having a little difficulty coming up with the ending."

"Hell, you know the ending," Rachel replied, only a few decibels softer. "You're a romance author—one of the best in the world. All romances have a happily-ever-after ending. Write it and send me the manuscript. We're weeks off schedule. Your fans are clamoring for their next Ellenore fix."

"Okay, will do," Ellenore replied meekly. In the five years Rachel had been her agent, Ellenore had never heard her so angry or frustrated. She was about to say something else when she heard the click on the other end.

She hung up the phone and stared at the blank computer screen, her gaze slowly drifting over to the manuscript box next to it—as empty as her head had been for weeks. *Where in the hell are you, Calli? I don't even care. You're my muse, and I need you to get your sweet ass back here. Now!*

AS ELLENORE STROLLED the few blocks from her house to the wine store, she thought about the last few years. It had been a good run—more than just a run. It had lasted close to five years, ever since she'd found her muse lying on her doorstep. Since then, her writing career had soared from a nobody to a some-

4

body and eventually to one of the top romance writers in the world. Early in the process, she'd acquired Rachel, a top literary agent who had helped her polish that first book around, then orchestrated a bidding war that Avon had eventually won.

Those had been good years, amazing years, years when she and her muse had churned out book after book, averaging at least four per year like clockwork. The muse had been a mysterious addition to her life. Even though Ellenore had come to think of it as male after finding it in bed with a lioness, it also had many feminine traits, so Ellenore eventually named it Calli after the Greek muse, Calliope. Ellenore had been ecstatic with her success. So had Rachel, as they both became quite well off financially while doing something that they both loved. And Calli had appeared quite content as well...until. It had started with Calli complaining about needing some time off, but Ellenore kept countering with, "Let's just get this book wrapped up first." By the time that had happened, Rachel would be back on the phone asking her for the next one and then the next and the next.

Then one morning, Ellenore had gone to her home office to resume her workday, only to find the daybed where Calli slept empty. A thorough search of the house and grounds confirmed Ellenore's worst fears. Calli had disappeared. That had been weeks ago. Since then, Ellenore had tried to start the next novel working from the few notes she had, but nothing was good enough. She began having nightmares of a blank computer screen chasing her down the street, followed closely behind by an empty manuscript box. It wasn't long afterward that she started making frequent trips to the wine store.

THE DRINKING HAD STARTED with just a glass or two at the end of a successful day of writing, but lately, the wine consumption had increased as the word production dried up. Wine Time, as she affectionately called it, had moved from starting at five-thirty to five, then four. Now, anytime she felt the icy fingers of fear threatening to catapult her into an anxiety attack, she'd excuse herself to the kitchen and her stash of Merlot or Cabernet. The wine had moved from a simple pleasure to a necessary painkiller and antidepressant.

As she walked the now familiar path from the wine store to her home, she pulled out one of the bottles from the paper bag. She had started buying at least one bottle with a screw top instead of a cork, so she didn't have to wait until she returned home to quiet her nerves. She glanced around to see if any of her neighbors might be watching, then chuckled. Really, what did she care what her neighbors thought? They already viewed her as the weirdo at the end of the street. You know, the one who's made a fortune pretending she knows everything about love and romance. She raised the bottle high above her head as she twisted it open. "Here's to what I think of your opinions!" She lowered the bottle to her lips and took several large gulps, then wiped her mouth with her sleeve.

"That's telling them!"

A shocked Ellenore turned in the direction of the voice. *Shit! I thought I was alone.* There, standing a few yards behind her, was her old friend, Allison. She'd not seen Allison in years, not since Ellenore's muse had appeared and Ellenore had accused Allison of channeling her not-so-dearly departed mother, who always found something derogatory to say about Ellenore.

"What are you doing here?" Ellenore asked.

"It looks like you could use a friend right about now," Allison replied. "Can I have a sip of that?" she asked, pointing to the bottle.

"You may not!" Ellenore said as she turned to resume her walk home.

She trudged on in silence, guzzling the wine as she went.

"So, you're going to give your old friend the silent treatment," Allison said, as Ellenore neared her home. "Is that the smartest move you can make?"

Ellenore continued walking, increasing the pace.

"I'd say you need a friend right about now, and as far as I can tell, I'm it. Well, me and that bottle."

"Leave the bottle out of it."

"Sure thing. Drink away. Fine by me."

Ellenore took another long pull on the now almost empty bottle. As she did so, Allison faded slowly away.

THE WEEKS SLID INTO a month, and then a second one. Ellenore still had no manuscript to send to Rachel, who was becoming increasingly belligerent with her former all-star author. During this time, Allison continued to make periodic appearances, most often after Ellenore was well into her second bottle of wine. Ellenore finally decided to forgive her old friend and since then, had started to appreciate the company.

On one such night as the two of them sat around the kitchen table, Ellenore broke one of her few remaining cardinal rules and opened a third bottle of wine for the day. She told Allison her plan. "I think I just need to come clean with Rachel. Go to her and let her know that my imagination has dried up. Maybe she can give me some ideas what I can do about it."

"Really? That's the best you can come up with?" Allison replied, a look of disgust on her face. "That's a terrible idea. She'll drop you like a hot potato, and then where will you be? No, I have a better idea. Do you want to hear it?"

Ellenore started to pour another glass of wine from the new bottle, then, realizing the glass wouldn't hold still, took a swig straight from the bottle. "I guess."

"How many books have you written and had published?" Before Ellenore could answer, Allison rushed on. "Dozens, right? All romances and all have done well. You've got everything that you need right there on your computer."

Ellenore, who was having trouble focusing on her friend's words, asked, "I do?"

"Sure you do. Listen, all you need to do is take one of those old stories and use it as a template for this next one. Change the names of the characters, maybe a few details about them. Change the setting a bit if you want. But it's all there. You don't need any imagination that way."

Ellenore thought about Allison's idea. Could it be that simple? Just take an old story and change the names and setting. Slowly, she started to shake her head. "No, that wouldn't be right. That would be like plag...plager...plagiarizing my own work," she said, then hiccuped.

"Who cares? Your readers won't. Neither will Rachel. Just give them what they want—another piece of drivel that'll make them happy."

"I don't know...it's just not right." Ellenore mumbled as she lowered her head to the table. "Not right...not right..." she repeated over and over as she drifted off to sleep.

She awoke the next morning with a stiff neck from her head resting on the kitchen table at an odd angle. She rubbed her eyes in an effort to clear them as she stumbled up to make a pot of coffee. She dumped in a couple extra scoops of her strongest brand. "Caffeine! I need caffeine!" she shouted to the walls and immediately regretted it. The top of her head felt like it would pop off like a champagne cork and shoot around the room. As the coffee began to percolate, she walked into the bathroom to relieve herself and to soak her head in a sink of cold water before returning to the kitchen.

She poured herself a mug of coffee, forgoing the customary sugar and cream. She needed it straight today. She wished she could administer it intravenously, but by mouth would have to do. She glanced at the microwave clock as it clicked over to 9:00 AM. Before she could get to the phone to take it off the hook, it rang. Ellenore groaned. It had to be Rachel, calling for the umpteenth time to ask about the manuscript. *I should just let it go to the answering machine,* she thought, but finally picked it up on the fourth ring.

"Good morning, Rachel," Ellenore began. "I know you're probably wondering where the manuscript is..." As she talked, she sifted through her mental rolodex of excuses trying to find one she hadn't already used.

"I'm sorry, this isn't Rachel. This is Melissa, from First Federal. Is this Ellenore Michner?"

"Oh, I'm sorry. Yes, this is she."

Good morning, Ms. Michner. You've been such a loyal customer of our bank I thought it only right that I alert you to a situation with your checking account."

"Situation? What situation? What's wrong?" Ellenore felt her heart skip a beat. She hadn't received a call from her bank in over five years, though before that time, she'd been on a first name basis with several bank officers from bouncing so many checks. Finally, she'd been forced to switch banks. Thankfully, since that time, she rarely even thought about her account. There was always plenty of money in it.

"A couple of your auto-pay bills didn't clear," the woman replied. "Since this is the first time it's happened, we can waive the penalty fee, but I thought you'd want to know. Would you like us to transfer some funds from your savings account?"

"Yes, yes, please do," Ellenore replied. "I'm so sorry. I had no idea the account was that low." Last time she'd checked, she'd had over a three thousand dollar balance, but how long ago had that been? She couldn't remember.

"No problem, Ms. Michner. Such things happen from time to time." *How well I know,* Ellenore thought. She remembered many a night as a child watching her mother sitting at her small corner desk fretting about how to 'pay too many bills with not enough money'. How many times had she heard her mother say that lament? *Oh my god, I'm turning into my mother! The hell you say,* she countered. *I'll be damned if I'll let that happen and especially not around my finances. I have to do something and do it quick.*

She hung up the phone and went to pour herself another mug of coffee, adding a little cream and sugar to this one. She sat at the table and pondered her plight. By the time the phone rang again ten minutes later, she'd made up her mind. As she suspected, the second call was from her agent.

"Rachel, I have some excellent news..." She paused, listening to Rachel, then continued. "I know I've said that before, but this time I mean it. I've had a breakthrough. Now, I haven't finished the manuscript yet, but I promise I'll have it to you by the end of the week. You can bank on it."

"I sure hope you're telling me the truth this time," Rachel said. "I can't keep putting the folks at Avon off. It's my reputation on the line as well as yours."

"I know, I know," Ellenore replied. "Don't worry. Just give me to the end of the week, and the finished manuscript will be in your inbox."

Ellenore hung up the phone, picked up her mug of coffee and strolled into her office, feeling good for the first time in weeks. She sat down and opened her laptop. As she waited for it to wake up, she went over the various stories in her mind she'd written in the past ten years. By the time the word processor had finished opening, she knew which story she'd use. As the day progressed, she found herself being very thankful to whoever had created the "Find and Replace" command.

Four days later the manuscript was finished, a full day ahead of schedule. She started a new email message in her email program, attached the file to it and mailed it to Rachel. Her hand hesitated for just a moment over the send button. Was she really going to follow through with Allison's plan? She remembered the embarrassing conversation with the lady from the bank. *Damn right I am*, she thought as she clicked on the send button. *Done. Time to celebrate with a glass of wine.* It turned out to be a bottle-and-a-half celebration.

THE NEXT MORNING THE jangling of the phone next to her bed awoke Ellenore, who had managed to weave herself into her bedroom before collapsing into a deep sleep bordering on a coma. As she instinctively reached for the phone, she gazed at the clock: 9:05. Could it be the bank calling again? She prayed not as she lifted the receiver from its cradle.

"Good morning." Her voice sounded like a creaking door resisting being opened. She cleared her throat and tried again. "Good morning."

"Yes, it is a good morning," Rachel said in an exuberant voice. "I just wanted to call to thank you for making my day, my week. I was so thrilled to see your email and with a file attached. I'll get right to it. I've already contacted Avon to let them know I have the manuscript in hand. You know what they said?" Ellenore opened her mouth to answer, but Rachel answered her own question first. "When will she start on the next one?" Rachel laughed, and after a moment's hesitation, Ellenore joined her. So, Allison's idea was going to work. In fact, it seemed to be working like a charm. She sat up in bed and stretched, holding the phone in the crook of her neck. There was a long silence on the other end of the line.

"Well, when will you get me the next one?" Rachel's tone had suddenly turned serious.

Ellenore didn't know how to answer the question. As far as she was concerned, Allison's idea had been a one-time thing, a desperate attempt to keep her career intact and the wolves from her door. Suddenly, Allison appeared, lying in bed beside her. "Go ahead. It worked like a charm, just as I said it would, and it'll work again."

Ellenore stared at her friend for several seconds before finally turning her attention back to the phone. "I've...I feel like I've had a real breakthrough in my creativity, Rachel. I'm sure I'll be able to get a new story to you in the next couple of months."

"Really? Awesome!" Rachel replied. "That would be great. After all, we've some lost ground to make up. Okay, I'll get right to reading this one, and you get to writing the next one." With that, the line went dead.

Ellenore stared at the phone in her hand, then breathed a sigh of relief. She'd finally made her agent happy again.

HER ELATION AND RELIEF didn't last long. In fact, it lasted less than a day. It ended in the late afternoon when she received another call from her agent. She was in the kitchen getting ready to start dinner when the phone rang. She glanced at the caller ID to see that it was Rachel calling again. Probably just calling to give her high praise for the manuscript, Ellenore thought as she picked up the phone.

"Hi Rachel, what's up?" Ellenore said in a light and airy voice.

There was a pause on the other end, then, "Are you sure you want me to send this manuscript on to Avon?"

"Sure, why not?" Ellenore replied, her mood taking a nose dive into the pits of hell. "Don't you like it?"

"Yes, I like it fine," Rachel said. "I liked it the first time I read it...over five years ago."

Suddenly Allison popped in behind Ellenore. "Deny, deny, deny."

Ellenore turned on her with a look of worry that quickly turned to one of anger. "Shuddup!"

"What was that?" Rachel asked.

"Nothing," Ellenore replied. "My next-door-neighbor is calling me. I think she may have fallen again. Let me call you back." Ellenore hung up the phone before Rachel had a chance to reply.

"She knows."

"Well, she might suspect," Allison said.

"No, she knows. Hell, I should have known better than to use that first book. That's the one that I originally sent to her. Of course she'd recognize it. She and I worked on it quite a bit before she shopped it around."

"Yeah, that was probably a dumb move," Allison agreed.

Ellenore glared at her. "This was your idea in the first place."

"Yeah, and it was a good one," Allison countered. "But even a good idea poorly executed turns into a bad idea. You're the one who chose the wrong book. You can't expect me to think of everything."

Ellenore picked up an empty wine bottle sitting on the counter next to her and flung it at Allison, who promptly disappeared in a puff of smoke as the bottle shattered against the far wall.

"THE TRUTH WILL SET you free...but first, it'll piss you off."

It was Calli's voice, coming from the other end of the bedroom where he stood leaning against the door frame. He wore a silly hat on his head that contrasted with the flowered shirt and lei around his neck. His ensemble was completed with a pair of baggy shorts and flip-flops.

"Where in hell have you been?" Ellenore shouted at him before jumping out of bed to give him a big hug, but he held up a hand to stop her. "Uh, uh, not yet. I'm not really here. You're dreaming."

Ellenore stopped in her tracks, "Dreaming? Really? Well, that would at least explain that silly outfit you're wearing."

Calli looked hurt. "Well, this is what I'm wearing at the moment. I said you're sleeping. I didn't say anything about my level of consciousness. Anyway," he said, waving one hand to change the subject, "did you hear what I said or were you still too asleep?"

"Yeah, I heard," Ellenore replied, annoyed by the question. "Something about telling the truth or pissing on the truth." She paused to consider what she'd said. "No, I guess I didn't hear what you said."

"The truth will set you free...but first, it'll piss you off," Calli repeated.

Ellenore considered the statement for a moment. "Okay, what am I supposed to do with that bit of fortune cookie wisdom?"

"How about applying it to the situation you're in? The situation that lying has dumped you into."

"What? You think I should tell Rachel the truth?" Ellenore asked, anger growing in her voice. "I can't do that. It would be career suicide."

"Well, here's the pissed off part coming through loud and clear. You can't or won't?"

"Take your choice," Ellenore answered. "It's all the same. I'm not."

"Okay," Calli replied in a calm voice. "It's your life. By the way, Hawaii is beautiful this time of the year." And with that, he faded away like the Cheshire Cat with his silly smile being the last thing to disappear.

ELLENORE SPENT THE next forty-eight hours in a living hell. Rachel continued to call her several times a day; her calls interspersed with calls from the bank as well as from several creditors. Frustrated, she unplugged the phone but found little solace in the silence that followed. Her mind continued to berate her without ceasing. Finally, she decided to walk to the store to buy some more liquid anesthetic.

As she walked, Calli's phrase continued to haunt her. As she passed the playground, she saw Allison once more, jumping rope. She tried to stroll quickly past, but her former friend saw her and joined her in the walk despite Ellenore's attempts to ignore her.

"Slow down. I want to talk to you," Allison said, as she huffed and puffed behind her.

"Well, I don't want to talk to you," Ellenore replied without bothering to turn around.

"But I know how you can get out of this mess you created."

Ellenore stopped and whirled around. "That I created? You've got to be kidding!"

"Okay, okay. Maybe I played some part in this," Allison conceded, "but don't you want to hear my idea how you can get out of it?"

"I'm not sure I do," Ellenore replied, but with less confidence. *After all, I don't have a clue what I'm going to do. What's the harm in listening?* "Okay, I guess. What's your idea?"

"It's straightforward. Tell Rachel to send the manuscript in and keep her mouth shut about it. Otherwise, you'll find another agent to represent you."

"That's your idea? Just keep perpetuating the lie?"

"Listen, you're Ellenore Michner, one of the most prolific and popular romance writers in the world. There are plenty of agents who'd jump at the chance to skim their ten to fifteen percent off the top." When Ellenore didn't say anything, Allison asked, "Well, what do you think?"

"I think you're a royal pain in the ass," Ellenore replied, "and I want you to leave me alone so I can buy some wine." She opened the door to the wine store and entered, being sure to close the door with Allison on the other side. When she left with her bag of wine, Allison was nowhere to be seen. Good riddance, Ellenore thought as she twisted off the screw cap of the wine and took a long guzzle.

But she only drank a few more swallows of the wine on her way home. Calli's and Allison's words kept reverberating through her mind. What am I going to do? I can't keep putting off a decision. She had to tell Rachel something soon, and her creditors certainly wouldn't leave her alone. I have to make a decision, but what can I do?

"The truth will set you free...but first, it'll piss you off."

"The truth will set you free...but first, it'll piss you off."

"The truth will set you free...but first, it'll piss you off."

"Leave me alone, Calli!" Ellenore screamed as she ran down the street in an effort to get away from Calli's voice blasting away in her mind.

Arriving home, she poured herself a glass of wine and meandered around the rooms of her home. Her once beautiful home had somehow mysteriously transformed into a pig sty. Everywhere she looked, all she could see was an assortment of dirty clothes (she didn't know she owned so many), food-encrusted dishes, empty wine bottles and stacks of old newspapers and magazines. There was also a distinctive odor permeating through the air, like somewhere amongst the rubble she might find the decaying remains of a dead rat. She walked around each room in an effort to locate the source of the smell, only then realizing that the odor came from her own body. She couldn't remember the last time she'd taken a shower.

I can do something about that, she thought. She walked into the bathroom, disrobing as she went. She turned on the hot water and climbed in, lathering herself from head to toe. She continued to let the steamy water wash over her until she ran out of hot water. She climbed out and toweled herself off, feeling better by taking at least one decisive action. So, why stop there, she thought.

How about making another small step. She went outside, grabbed one of the empty garbage cans and re-entered the house. She cleaned and washed for the next three hours. Somewhere along the way she decided to dump all the wine as well.

She took a second, shorter shower before walking into her closet and putting on the brightest color dress she could find. It reminded her of Calli's Hawaiian shirt. She felt a pang of longing. She missed Calli more than she'd allowed herself to admit. Sure, he'd been the source of her creativity, but more than that. He'd been her best friend, someone she could count on to tell her the truth. But he had needed to get away. He'd tried numerous times to tell her that, but she'd ignored him. Finally, she'd left him no choice but to run away.

"I'm sorry, Calli. Really, I am." She sighed heavily. She looked around her. *Well, at least when my creditors come to haul my stuff away, they'll find a clean house*, she thought. *Now what? Time to confront the real issue I've been avoiding. What to do with the fake manuscript I sent to Rachel.*

She walked into the kitchen to place the call to Rachel's direct line. Keep breathing; she told herself as she listened to the phone ring. Rachel picked up on the third ring.

"Hello, Rachel, this is Ellenore."

"Well, it's about time you called me back," Rachel replied, unable to hide the anger in her voice.

"Yes, I know. I'm sorry. I just needed some time to think."

"And?"

"I've decided I want the manuscript sent..." Ellenore stopped to take a deep breath, "but not to Avon. Send it back to me or better yet, just delete it and forget I ever sent it, please."

After a long pause, Rachel replied. "Okay, I think that's a wise decision, Ellenore." In a softer voice, she continued. "What's going on, Ellenore? You've been one of my best authors, and I don't just mean most prolific and profitable. I've enjoyed your stories, and working with you has been most satisfying. That is, until lately. What happened?"

Ellenore felts the tears well up in her eyes and begin to stream down her face. She wiped them away from her face and sighed. She heard Calli's voice again: "The truth will set you free...." *That's all?* she thought. *How about the rest?* But nothing else came. She straightened her shoulders and spoke with more confidence than she felt. "Here's the situation. I've dried up. I've no more ideas for romance stories. I haven't had a decent idea in months. The longer it's gone, the worse it's gotten. Now I've got bills I can't pay, and still no fresh ideas. I thought I could doctor up one of my old stories, and it would bide me some time until my muse resurfaced, but you were right. That would be such a disservice to you, my readers, to Avon...and most of all, to me. So, send it back to me or at least delete it. Tell the folks at Avon, I'm sorry, but I won't be able to fulfill our contractual agreement."

There was a long pause on the other end of the line. Finally, Rachel said, in a hushed voice filled with compassion, "I'll delete the file, no worry. Just hang in there for a bit, Ellenore. Don't do anything rash. I'll be back in touch." And with that, she ended the call.

Ellenore hung up the phone and looked at her now clean kitchen. *Shit! No wine. Maybe I was a little rash in my cleaning,* she thought, but then again, maybe not. She didn't feel like wine. In fact, she felt surprisingly good. What was that feeling she felt? Could it be...

"Freedom," a voice said from behind her, but when she turned around, no one was there. *Voices in my head again,* she thought. *I am cracking up.* "Go to the playground," came the voice again. This time it was unmistakably Calli's voice she heard.

"The playground?" Ellenore asked, then remembered the playground she routinely passed on her way to the wine store. *Oh, what the hell? I may as well give in and do what it says. What else do I have to do at the moment?* She grabbed a jacket from the coat rack and walked out the door. On the way to the playground, she marveled at how good she felt. Could the voice have been right? Was this what freedom felt like? How could that be? She still didn't have a story idea, was about to ruin her career by breaking a contract with her publisher, not to mention the growing number of creditors clamoring for a piece of her skin. *But at least I still have my integrity,* she thought. *Well, let's be honest. I'm in the process of restoring my integrity, and that feels good.*

As she approached the playground, she saw a lone figure sitting on one end of the seesaw, moving slowly up and down as though there was a second person on the other end, but the other end was empty. Drawing closer, she recognized the colorful Hawaiian shirt and silly hat. It was Calli, come home at last! She ran over to the seesaw intending to give her muse a giant hug just before lambasting him for being gone so long, but he stopped her with a hand signal and pointed to the other end of the seesaw.

Ellenore reluctantly climbed on, and the two of them went up and down, up and down for a couple of minutes without either of them talking. Each time Ellenore opened her mouth to say something, Calli would put his index finger to his lips and hush her quiet. After another minute or two, she opened her mouth again. This time he smiled at her and nodded.

"Where have you been?" she asked.

"You know," he answered pointing with one hand at his shirt. "Vacationing in Hawaii."

"So that was really you in my dream?"

"Of course," he answered. "Just as it was really you on the phone confessing to Rachel."

"How did you know about that?"

Calli shrugged and smiled. "I have my ways."

After another couple of ups and downs, he asked, "What are your plans now?"

It was Ellenore's turn to shrug. "I don't know. I was hoping you could tell me." When he didn't say anything, she continued. "I'm thinking about getting a job, just until I get back on my feet. Something that would pay the bills and keep a roof over my head, little details like that."

Calli nodded. "Hmm, I guess that could work..." but he didn't sound convinced.

"You have a better idea?"

"Yes, as a matter of fact, I do." He held up one hand, and a book suddenly appeared in it.

"What's that?" Ellenore asked, then immediately felt stupid. It was apparent what it was.

"Your next book," Calli replied.

Ellenore stared at the book, trying to get a better look at the cover. "Really? But there aren't any bare-chested men or swooning women on the cover."

"That's because it's not a romance."

"Really? No kidding? But I don't know how to write anything but a romance."

"I know," Calli replied with a chuckle, "but I do. Trust me. This is going to be your best work yet...by a mile."

"My best work yet?" Ellenore repeated, then stared at him suspiciously. "What's it about?"

"It's about a young artist that loses her way and comes close to selling her soul to the devil, but at the last minute finds her way back. It's a real tearjerker, but with a happy ending. Interested?"

"Yeah, maybe," Ellenore smiled back at him. "Can we go home and talk about it?"

"Sure thing," Calli said as he floated off the seat of the seesaw while his end was on the ground. Ellenore gasped, expecting her end to come crashing down, but it too simply floated to the ground.

As the two of them entered Ellenore's home, she noticed the blinking light on her answering machine. *Probably just a bunch of creditors calling for their pound of flesh*, she thought, but decided to check it anyway. No point in trying to run away from her problems.

She was surprised to hear Rachel's voice on the recording instead. "Hi, Ellenore. Listen. I had to check with my business partner before I could share this with you. Several years ago, when we started the agency, we decided to set aside one percent of our earnings into an emergency fund. At the time, we thought it would be to help our business through challenging times, but we found that one of the best uses of the fund has been to help some of our loyal authors when they go through dry periods...like the one you're experiencing now. We want to support you through this spell, so give me a call back and let's see what you need." The recording clicked off.

Ellenore turned to Calli whose head was already deep inside the refrigerator. "Well, I'll be damned."

Calli straightened up, a chicken drumstick in one hand. "It's good to be home."

"It's great to have you home," Ellenore agreed. "Any more chicken in there?"

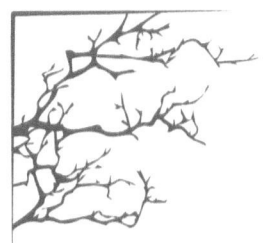

GOLDCRAFT

❝ Youth is the most beautiful thing in this world—and what a pity that it has to be wasted on children!❞ George Bernard Shaw

Randall Dixon turned to look back at the other biker, prepared to yell at him to hurry up, until he noticed his younger brother's flushed face dripping sweat and his heavy panting. Instead, he slowed his pace and waited for Pee Wee to catch up. Of course, Pee Wee wasn't his brother's real name, but it's what everyone had called him pretty much from his first day on Earth when he'd been born four weeks premature. Randall had asked his brother once if he minded being called Pee Wee, to which he answered, "No, why should I? It's my name, isn't it? It's sure better than Maurice. What were Mom and Dad thinking?"

"We're almost there," Randall said as he wiped his own face with the back of his hand. "Want to race the last block?"

"Sure," Pee Wee replied between labored breaths. "Last...one...there..." The challenge took too much energy—energy he'd need to beat his older brother.

Randall did the best he could to make sure the race ended in a dead heat and didn't protest when Pee Wee claimed victory. Even though Pee Wee was about to turn eleven, most people thought there was more than three years difference between the boys. Not only was he small for his age, he'd always been sickly, catching just about every cold or flu that was in the area, each time being hit harder than anyone else.

Even so, there was no mistaking that the two boys were brothers—same jet black hair, same deep blue eyes, same winning smile. Also, they almost always hung out together. It wasn't just that Randall took being the older brother to heart and felt a need to protect the small boy, but he also genuinely enjoyed his brother's company, his quick wit and his tenacious outlook on life.

The two boys placed their bikes in the bike rack and started walking down the street towards Goldcraft, Inc. Despite the "Inc." at the end of the name, the shop was small, hardly more than a narrow alleyway between two other buildings, but it was also one of the most interesting and well-kept shops along Foster Flat's Main Street. As far as anyone knew, Albert Goldman had owned the shop for...well, for as long as anyone could recall. It had been a mainstay of Main Street for decades. But it had been the eclectic mixture of merchandise found in the display window that had first attracted the two brothers. Everything from old pocket watches to jewel-encrusted pendants in the shape of bugs and the models of three-masted sailing ships that regally sat in the upper display.

As Randall pushed the shop door open, the bell tinkled, alerting the owner that a new customer had arrived. Goldman glanced up from his workbench to peer at the two boys who were undoubtedly some of his youngest visitors. He slid the magnifying loupe onto his forehead and smiled.

"Ahh, it is only you, my fine friends. I was hoping for a paying customer for a change but come in, come in. Perhaps others will see you in my shop and realize I'm open."

It was pretty much the same greeting he always used whenever the Dixon brothers visited, but as far as Randall could tell, Mr. Goldman's business was doing just fine. He never saw the old man when he wasn't working on some watch or piece of jewelry. He glanced around at the walls, where a line of wild animal heads hung.

"Is there something new on the wall?" Randall asked.

"Yes, you're quite observant," Goldman replied, pointing to the head of a mountain goat with large curving horns. "It came in a couple days ago. Do you like it?"

"Impressive," Randall said.

"Yeah, it's cool," Pee Wee replied as he walked over to take a closer look. "Are those horns real?"

"That they are, boy. How'd you like to get butted by one of those?"

"No, thanks," Pee Wee said as he backed away a couple steps. He looked above where Goldman sat and pointed to the large black bear that stood in the corner of the balcony. "Yogi is still my favorite."

"Mine, too," Goldman replied with a chuckle. He sat back in his chair and rubbed the bridge of his nose. "What are you boys up to today?"

"Aw, nothing," Randall replied. "Just hanging out, you know."

"And how are your studies? Have you brought that spelling grade up yet?" he asked, gazing at Pee Wee.

"Yeah, I think so. We had a pop quiz on Monday and I made a B on it."

"Good for you. And you, boy. How's the history coming along?" Goldman asked, turning his gaze on Randall, who shrugged, but before he could answer, the bell over the front door jingled. He looked around to see a large brute of a man dressed in a tailored black suit with a formal bow tie pushing a smaller, much older man in a wheelchair. The man in the suit reminded Randall of Herman Munster about to go to a formal dinner. The man in the wheelchair had to be the oldest person he'd ever seen. It was hard to imagine someone could be so withered and wrinkled and still be alive, but indeed he was. The man held a large wooden chest on his lap, his hands gripping it as though it were his most valuable possession.

"Ahh, Mr. McMasters. What are you doing here today? I believe our appointment isn't until next week," Goldman said as he rose from his chair, noticeably flustered by the appearance of the two men.

"I couldn't wait," the old man replied in a dry voice, hardly above a whisper. "I had to see you this week. Don't worry. I'll make it worth your while." He patted the chest to emphasize his point.

"Well, okay then," Goldman replied. He pointed behind him towards the rear of the shop. "Please, right this way. I'll be with you in a moment."

McMasters nodded and waved his companion forward with a skeleton-like hand.

When the two were gone, Randall looked at his friend, who appeared more worried, even frightened, than he'd ever seen him. "Is everything all right?"

"Yes, of course," Goldman replied, though his face didn't match the words. "He just caught me by surprise. Everything will be fine...just fine, I'm sure." But it sounded to Randall like Goldman was trying to convince himself. "I'm afraid we'll have to cut our visit short today," Goldman continued. "Come again next week. I always enjoy your visits."

"Sure thing," Pee Wee replied. "You're pretty cool, yourself...for an old guy."

Randall threw his brother a displeased look, but Goldman only chuckled.

Not far from home, Randall pulled to the side of the road and stopped, waiting for Pee Wee to catch up. Together they walked their bikes up the last hill before reaching their mountain home. It had become a ritual of theirs. The five or ten minutes it took to reach the top of the hill gave them time to re-cap the day and review whatever adventures they might have shared. It also gave Pee Wee a few minutes to recuperate before entering the house and facing their mother with the number one question she always asked. "Are you okay, Pee Wee? You look a little…" Fill in the blank. Most commonly the sentence ended with something like peeked, or flushed, or tired, or pale, or like you may be run-ning a fever. She never seemed at a loss to find new ways to describe her younger son's appearance and it was never good.

Randall walked slowly to give Pee Wee plenty of time to rest and prepare himself for their overly concerned mother. Finally, he asked, "What do you think that man wanted with Mr. Goldman?"

"I don't know," Pee Wee replied in a soft, whispery voice as he continued to catch his breath.

"Did you notice how Mr. Goldman reacted?"

"Yeah," Pee Wee replied.

"What do you think was in the box?"

Pee Wee paused to consider the question before replying. "Maybe a shrunk-en head, or a pirate's treasure."

"Yeah." Randall smiled. "Or maybe the pirate's shrunken head with his trea-sure."

The two boys looked at each other in the rapidly disappearing light of an-other day and both shuddered. It was a favorite game they liked to play, scaring each other with tall tales of pirates and witches and such.

"Grownups are so weird sometimes," Randall said as he started walking again.

"Yeah, like always," Pee Wee agreed.

As soon as the two boys left, Goldman walked to the door, locked it, and placed the closed sign on the door's window before limping back to the rear of the store. He found McMasters sitting in his wheelchair with the chest still in his lap and Helgor, his valet, standing behind him.

"Where have you been and why haven't you been in touch before now?" Goldman asked, surprised at how angry he'd become between the door and the rear office. "How long has it been? Twenty years? Longer?"

"Twenty-seven to be exact," McMasters replied, apparently nonplussed by Goldman's reaction. "My businesses had a series of unexpected setbacks. I didn't keep the appointment because I couldn't live up to my part of the agreement, but I can now." He patted the chest once again.

"Well, you could have at least called or written me a letter...something," Goldman replied in a strained but calmer voice. "I thought you had died, maybe killed in an auto accident or something. I kept checking the newspapers, but nothing."

"Yeah, well, I'm fine now and ready to resume our agreement," McMasters replied. "There's enough gold here to buy back my youth. Let's see, I think thirty years should do nicely."

Goldman stared at him, his mouth falling open in shock disbelief. "Are you crazy? I don't keep that amount of youthful energy around. The most I've ever had on hand at any one time was nine or ten years, and that was back when I had a larger clientele of young men and women willing to sell off a year or two of their lives for start up capital or to pay off a gambling debt or take care of medical bills for a loved one."

McMasters sat staring at him for several seconds, anger growing in his eyes as he tapped lightly on the chest with his fingers. "Well, how much do you have?"

"I don't know exactly. I'd have to check. Maybe six or seven years worth," Goldman replied.

"Well, that will never do," McMasters shot back. "You'll just have to acquire some more...at least twenty years more."

Goldman chuckled dryly. "It's not that easy. It's not like I can hop on down to the local superstore and pick up two cases of youthfulness. I mean, I can check around with some of my other clients to see if they'd be willing to part with a bit more, but..."

"Enough!" McMasters suddenly shouted, startling the other two men who both jumped at the word. "I need it all and I need it now. I'm running out of time. Look at me. No one should have to put up with this much old age. I can hardly walk. I'm down to little more than a hundred and twenty pounds soaking wet, which, by the way, speaking of wet, I do that to myself way too often. I want my youth back. I've got the money for it and I'm here to buy it per our long-standing agreement. Besides, it looks like you could use a little of your own. I know that's how this works. You keep a small percentage of what you take in. It's only fair. It's the price of doing business. So, when can you make arrangements so we can complete this transaction?"

"You don't understand. It's not that easy. It could take me years to acquire that much..."

"No, no, no, no," McMasters interrupted again. He took a couple deep breaths, but continued to tap nervously on the chest. Finally, he said, "Let me see if I can be a little clearer. I'll give you ten days to come up with your side of the deal. At least twenty-seven years worth. Preferably all thirty. If, upon my return, you don't have it, I'll be forced to show you why I keep such a large valet under my employment. Do you understand me? And after Helgor is through playing with you, I'll go around this fine little town and let everyone know exactly what a shady business you've been running here. You'll be ruined. Washed up."

"But where in the world could I possibly get that much in such a short time?"

"That's your problem," McMasters replied. "Figure it out." He nodded to Helgor. "Let's go."

Helgor started pushing him towards the door, but before they reached it, McMasters raised his hand.

"Those two kids that were in the shop when I arrived could be a good starting point. Use your imagination...just get me what I require."

After McMasters left, Goldman stood glaring at the door. *The nerve of some people*, Goldman thought. *Stays gone for close to three decades and then saunters in making ridiculous demands, then threatens to have me beaten up and ruin my life if I don't comply. The nerve!* At the same time, he knew McMasters wasn't joking around and would be more than willing to follow through with the threat. People at the end of their lives often became ornery and unreasonable, especially those accustomed to wealth and power.

Finally, Goldman walked over to the old puppet stage that he now used for storage. He paused for a moment to gaze at the half dozen lifelike puppets that hung from the sides of the stage. Puppeteering had once been Goldman's passion but he'd abandoned the hobby several years ago. When Randall and Pee Wee had first seen the stage and puppets, they'd pleaded with him for a show. He'd put them off, claiming his arthritis made it too painful to perform so they had eventually dropped the request.

He walked around to the rear of the stage. Stooping down, he unlocked one of the side storage drawers and pulled it open to reveal five spherical globes about the size of a large goose egg. Only one of them glowed with a soft golden sheen, the dull gray color of the other four indicating they were empty vessels ready to be filled with youthful energy. He estimated from the gold color that the one globe was a little over half full. He'd been saving it for himself but now he was faced with a much more serious problem. How to fill it and at least two more of them within the next ten days.

He pushed the drawer closed and locked it before making his way back to the front where he once more locked the door that McMasters and his goon had left open. He turned around to gaze at the small shop that was now in jeopardy of being closed forever. His eyes fell on the line of animal heads along one wall. Besides the newly acquired mountain ram was the head of a deer with a full rack, two pheasants in the midst of flight, a large mouth bass and the head of a lynx. A large and well-preserved raccoon caught in the motion of cleaning its face with his human-like hands sat on the display case below the other animals.

"What am I to do?" Goldman asked out loud, dismayed by the pleading sound of the question.

After several seconds, he heard the reply. "It is indeed a problem, but I'm sure if we put all our heads together, we can come up with a solution," answered the deer, who then looked from side to side at his companions, who all nodded. Even the large bear, who'd been affectionately named Yogi by the Dixon boys, nodded agreement.

"We all have something at stake here," the black bear said. "We certainly don't want to see our benefactor beaten up, and if your secret is revealed, the townsfolk are likely to torch the place."

Goldman groaned, the image of his shop in flames flashing across his mind.

The group spent the next several minutes brainstorming ideas. The raccoon proposed turning McMasters in to the authorities, but everyone agreed it would be too easy for the man to simply deny the accusation and in the process, the police would likely question Goldman's sanity. The suggestion of closing up the shop with a 'gone on vacation' sign on the door was also quickly nixed.

Finally, Yogi spoke up. "Why not do what McMasters suggested?"

"What?" Goldman asked. "He suggested I use the youth of the Dixon boys. I couldn't do that. They're my friends, not to mention Pee Wee's health is too poor. He'd never survive it. That's the worst idea yet, Yogi."

"Well, that's not exactly what I meant," the bear replied. "I'm very fond of Randall and Pee Wee as well. After all, they're the ones that gave me my name. But, they have friends in school, right? And those friends have other friends. Why not gather a bunch of the kids together and pull a little youth from all of them. That way no one is hurt, McMasters gets his youth back, and we go on living our lives."

"Why, that's just too absurd," the raccoon replied. "Who ever heard of such a thing?"

The bear opened his mouth to argue, but before he could say anything, Goldman spoke up. "You know, that might just work."

"Really?" the raccoon asked. "Are you serious? You really think it would work?"

"Maybe," Goldman said. "I'm not sure how exactly, but the general idea has possibilities. I mean, desperate times call for desperate actions. The question is how do we attract a large group of kids in just the next ten days, especially without drawing the attention of the rest of the townsfolk?"

"You aren't seriously considering this crazy bear's suggestion, are you?" the raccoon asked.

"Do you have a better idea?" Goldman shot back.

"Well, no, not at the moment," the raccoon said.

"Then let's explore this one further. How can we attract, I don't know, say thirty or forty kids to one location before the deadline?"

There was a long pause again as Goldman and most of the animals tried to come up with an answer, while the raccoon huffed and snuffed his disgruntlement. Finally, the bear said, "I've got it. Hold a puppet show!"

The raccoon was quick to reply. "What a dumb..."

"Hush, Rocky," Goldman interrupted. "A puppet show?"

"Yeah. You've got everything you need in the back, right? And Randall and Pee Wee have pleaded with you to do a show, and you've kept putting them off. Well, now seems to be the perfect time. They can tell all their friends to come. There's not a lot to do in Foster Flat, especially during the summertime. I bet we can easily get the number of kids we'll need."

Although he wasn't sure, Goldman thought he could hear the puppets in the back all clapping their approval.

"Can we come?" the deer asked.

"Yeah, this will be so much fun," one of the pheasants added and the rest of the animals all nodded, even Rocky.

"Well, maybe," Goldman replied. He looked around at the shop. It was long and narrow but with a little rearranging, he could easily fit thirty or more kids in the front room if they all sat on the floor. It would also save him needing to find another location. He only had ten days to pull this off, but with a little help from his two friends, that should be enough time.

But what about Pee Wee? He was already so sickly. What would the spell needed do to him? Somehow, Goldman would have to persuade Randall to keep his brother away. He would promise them a private showing. That would do the trick. At least he hoped it would.

Goldman peeked through the makeshift curtain at the flock of fluttering and fidgeting children ranging in age from preschool to Randall's age. *So much youthful energy*, he thought. Surely, none of them would miss it or be adversely affected if he simply borrowed (okay, stole) a little from each of them. Somehow, he and his two small assistants had managed to pull it all together with almost a full day to spare. He studied the faces one last time to be sure Randall had done his job and kept Pee Wee away. Randall said his brother had been deeply disappointed when he was told he couldn't attend and then turned to anger in an attempt to get his way.

"I worked as hard as anyone to make this happen," Pee Wee had complained, "and now you're telling me I can't be there. That's just not fair."

Goldman had to agree it wasn't fair, but it was the way it had to be. The offer of a private showing had only partially eased his disappointment, but at least it had worked—no Pee Wee in the audience. He'd just have to find another way to make amends with his little friend.

Meanwhile, it was time to get on with it. Time to steal a little bit of youth from the children of Foster Flat while praying none of their parents ever found out what he'd done. How would he ever make it up to these boys and girls? Of course, no one would ever know what had happened. He had it all set up for the transfer spell to be included in the show. They'd all be asked to participate, like in Peter Pan where everyone is encouraged to clap to save Tinker Bell's life.

Except, in this case, they'd be invited to close their eyes and dream of their most heartfelt desire. Then, everyone would fall into a deep sleep for a few minutes while the transfer took place, and the crystal globes hidden behind the front of the puppet stage would begin to glow as they were filled with youthful energy.

Later, he would take a small portion for himself, for that was the deal and how he had managed to live for so many years. Truth be told, it was the only reason he continued his behind-the-scenes business. Like so many of his clients, he'd become addicted to living.

Goldman took his position behind the stage and gave Randall the signal to raise the curtain. The first scene was all his and would give his assistant time to get in place for the next part. Randall had been a quick study, and Goldman made sure to keep the storyline simple so no more than two puppets would be on stage at any one time. Everything went like clockwork, just as they had practiced it, until just after the closing scene. The climactic scene with the magic spell had gone flawlessly and Goldman felt confident that enough youth had been transferred to the globes to satisfy the contract.

The entire crowd stood up for a standing ovation, clapping and hooting their praise until someone suddenly shouted, "What's wrong with that little girl?" Everyone turned in the direction the boy was pointing. Goldman held his breath, then let it out when he realized the girl in question was simply sleeping. He started to relax but as he continued to stare, he felt an ominous feeling building in the pit of his stomach. Something wasn't quite right. Then he realized it was the little girl's hair. It didn't sit quite right on her head. In the next moment, he knew why. The hair was a wig and the little girl wasn't a girl at all. It was Pee Wee—imaginative, tenacious Pee Wee. He'd found a way to see the show. Goldman hoped the boy's ingenuity hadn't cost him his life.

For the next twenty-four hours, Goldman felt trapped in a living nightmare as concerned parents appeared from every corner of the town, along with questions from the police and members of the school board. It became vividly clear to him that where Foster Flat's children were concerned, it was ill advised to do anything that might put them in harm's way. Luckily, Randall came to his friend's defense several times, especially when his distraught mother showed up at Goldman's shop. The ambulance had just left to take Pee Wee to the hospital as the medics continued their effort to rouse him from a deep sleep.

It was fortunate that Goldman had a stellar reputation in the town. Several of the other local shop owners assured Mrs. Dixon that he had meant no harm to anyone and especially not to Pee Wee. But the more people who came to his defense, the guiltier he felt, for he realized he really hadn't had the children's well being in mind when he'd conducted the puppet show, and now one of his dearest friends was in a coma because of it.

He tossed and turned that night, trying to come up with a way to fix the problem that he'd caused. He knew from personal experience that youthful energy had incredible healing properties. He would just need to figure out a way to siphon off a little of it and get it to Pee Wee before the small boy deteriorated further.

He was still in the midst of working out the details when McMasters showed up at his shop the following evening looking even older, with a gray pallor and a raspy breath.

"Do you have my order ready?" he asked, as Helgor pushed him into the shop.

"Yes," Goldman said.

"All of it?"

"Yes, all of it," Goldman replied, then added, "but given how long you've gone without a transfusion and your condition, I must insist you remain here tonight so I can monitor the process. Otherwise, I can't guarantee the outcome."

McMasters glared at him suspiciously a moment before replying. "I never needed to stay previously."

"You were never on death's door," Goldman started to say, but stopped himself at the last moment and said instead, "I realize that, but to infuse this amount into someone in such a frail condition as yours requires special care and attention. Otherwise, the treatment could overtax your heart."

McMasters continued studying Goldman for several seconds before finally nodding. "Oh, all right. I don't want to come this far just to have something go wrong at the last minute. Where do you want me?"

"Right here is fine," Goldman said with a sigh of relief. "I'll just lock up and pull the drapes so we won't be disturbed. By tomorrow morning you should be feeling much better and by the end of the month, your rejuvenation should be complete." *And if my plan goes smoothly, Pee Wee should be feeling better soon also*, Goldman thought.

He walked to the rear of the shop to fetch the storage globes. He'd spent much of the previous night poring over the ancient text he'd discovered decades ago in a used book store on an island in the Mediterranean. The book had eventually led him to his new profession. He'd finally found the key passage he'd been looking for; instructions on how to channel a small amount of the youthful energy into a fourth globe that he now placed in his pants pocket.

Before returning to McMasters, he paused for a moment to say a short prayer that all would go well. Unfortunately, his prayer went unanswered. Within the first few minutes of making the energy transfer, Goldman knew something was going wrong. He could feel the globe in his pocket beginning to heat up, a feeling that grew in intensity as the minutes passed. He tried to move in such a way to avoid contact with the sphere but all he managed to do was draw McMasters' attention.

"What's going on? What's that in your pocket?" the old man asked, pointing to the bulge that was now glowing dimly through the thin lining of his pocket.

"Oh, that? Nothing really," Goldman replied with a nervous tremble to his voice. "I'm...I'm just saving my commission for later."

"I don't believe you," McMaster replied. "Take it out of your pocket. Let me see it."

Reluctantly, Goldman reached into his pocket and withdrew the globe, holding it lightly in an effort to keep from burning himself further. He took a handkerchief from his back pocket and placed the globe on it.

"What are you doing?" McMasters asked, growing more suspicious by the moment. "Give that thing to Helgor."

"It's hot," Goldman said, pulling the globe away from the valet.

"Hot, is it?" McMasters sneered. "You're trying to steal from me, aren't you? You're grabbing more than your share."

"No, really," Goldman replied.

"Then why is it so hot? And why not simply take in your portion directly?"

"I can explain," Goldman said. "You see, there's this boy, one of the ones that were here on your last visit. He's in the hospital and needs my help. I need a little of the youthful energy to give to him."

"Oh, you do, do you?" McMasters spat back. "Isn't that a sweet story. It's also a bunch of bull. You should never try to con a con-man. Helgor, show our Mr. Goldman what happens when someone tries to take advantage of my generous nature. Start with his fingers and work up the arms."

As Helgor lumbered towards him, Goldman placed the globe behind his back in an act of defiance, but there was nowhere to go. He started to back away from the giant, but felt the edge of one of the display cases press along his back.

"Leave him alone."

"Yeah, pick on someone your own size."

"Step back."

Goldman's animal friends all shouted at the same time.

Confused by the sudden outburst, Helgor stopped, looking in the direction of the voices.

"What the hell is going on here?" McMasters shouted. "How in the world...?"

"Leave him alone," the deer repeated sternly from the wall.

McMasters continued to stare at the animals, a look of incredulity on his face. Then he laughed. "Good trick, Goldman, but it won't work. Go ahead, Helgor. Don't worry about them. They're all stuck to the wall."

Helgor took another step towards Goldman, who now had a smile on his face. Even though he spoke softly, Goldman's words resonated throughout the shop. "But they're not." He pointed to the bear and raccoon. As if on cue, the bear leapt onto Helgor as the raccoon flew through the air, landing on McMasters' head.

THE NEXT MORNING, ALBERT Goldman took a cab to the hospital to see Pee Wee. He carried with him a small vase of flowers filled with small pebbles in the bottom to give the stems a firm foundation. He was surprised and pleased to see Randall was there visiting with his younger brother, then realized it was Saturday. Randall was equally pleased to see his old friend.

"Please sit and stay a while," Randall said as he rose from the lone chair that sat next to the bed, offering it to Goldman.

Goldman shook his head. "No, I really can't stay long. I have to get back to the shop. It's in need of a good cleaning so I can open it for business later. How is he doing?"

"The doctors say he's stable, whatever that's supposed to mean," Randall replied, obviously worried about his little brother. "We're all trying to stay hopeful, but the longer he goes like this, the harder it is."

"I understand," Goldman replied as he placed the vase of flowers on the table next to Pee Wee's bed. "Don't give up hope. I had a dream last night that Pee Wee would be fine. It'll just take a little more time."

"Thanks, Mr. Goldman. I appreciate your words. How dependable are your dreams for coming true?"

"Very," Goldman replied, smiling at Randall. "Just give it a little more time. Now, I must get back to the shop." He turned to leave, but then stopped. "By the way, I'd like to start offering puppet shows regularly to the kids around here. It's time I started giving back." *Giving back what I stole*, he thought. "Do you think you two could help me with that?"

"Sure thing," Randall replied. "I'm sure Pee Wee would love to help." He glanced over to his sleeping brother with a look of affection that melted Goldman's heart.

It wasn't until late into Saturday evening when one of the night nurses noticed a warm golden glow coming from the flower vase. "What in the world?" she whispered, as she walked over to inspect it more closely. She was about to pick it up to go show it to the other nurses on the floor, but was interrupted by a soft cough, followed a moment later by a raspy voice coming from the bed.

"Where am I? Where's my brother?"

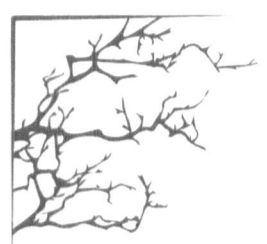

MASK MUSEUM

Daisy Davis catches the movement of the boy out the corner of her eye just in time to keep him from taking one of the hundreds of masks off the wall and placing it on his face.

"No, no," she says for what seems like the twentieth time. "You mustn't touch the masks and definitely don't put one on."

"Why not?" the tall, lanky toe-head of a boy asks, also for the twentieth time. "Isn't that what masks are for?"

"Not these masks," Daisy replies. At sixty-seven years of age, she finds she has little patience for such questions, Still, she takes a deep breath and slowly lets it out before replying in as calm a voice as she can muster. "It's considered bad luck to put on these ceremonial masks. Now, please, look but don't touch."

"Really? Bad luck," the know-it-all father replies. "I've never heard such a superstition."

And of course, if you haven't heard it, then it must not exist, right? Daisy thinks, but then bites her tongue to keep it to herself.

"Well, the African tribes where many of these masks came from believe that certain masks have the power to steal the soul of anyone who tries to wear them."

"Hogwash," the father replies as he walks over to his son and tousles his hair affectionately. "I think you made up that story just to scare little boys. Come on, Alice. I know when we're not welcome somewhere."

A young woman who was clearly the boy's mother and the source of his blonde hair nods and obediently follows her husband and son towards the door.

Daisy opens her mouth to object or apologize, she isn't sure which, but then closes it again. It's late in the day and she's ready to close the Mask Museum. She and her husband had founded the museum over twenty years ago after spending the first twenty-five years of their marriage traveling around the world collecting masks from dozens of different cultures.

The family turns to leave. The small house with blue siding and matching dark blue shutters doubles as the museum and Daisy's home. As they open the door, a slender young man wearing a wrinkled black blazer that hangs on his almost skeletal frame pushes his way around them. He's followed a moment later by a second, much larger man that reminds Daisy of Hoss Cartwright from the TV show, *Bonanza*. He has the same, happy, easygoing smile on his face while his companion wears an expression of sternness, even worry.

"I'm sorry, but the museum is closed for the day," Daisy says as she tries to block them from entering.

"Doesn't look closed to me," the slender man replies. "Come on, Moonpie. Look at the pretty masks." He speaks as though talking to a small child even though Moonpie is well over six feet tall and could no doubt play lineman for the Chicago Bears.

"Aww, Isaac. Can't you see the lady is tired and wants to go home?"

Daisy doesn't bother to point out that her home is less than twenty steps away.

"Maybe we should come back tomorrow."

"Look at these things," Isaac replies, ignoring his companion as well as Daisy. "These are some humdinger, ugly ass masks. I bet they're worth a fortune, don't you? Where'd you get all these things?" he asks, finally looking in Daisy's direction.

"My husband and I traveled around the world collecting them," Daisy replies, finding herself falling into a part of her tour speech despite herself. "There are over sixty countries represented, but never mind. Come back the first of the week. We're closed tomorrow and Monday, but come back Tuesday. I'll be happy to give you a tour."

"Where's your husband?" Isaac asks, ignoring her request and gazing around the room. "I'd like to meet him."

"He's no longer around," Daisy replies, automatically answering with the same vague response she always gives when asked the question.

"Ahh, that's sad," Moonpie says, frowning.

"We're just passing through," Isaac continues as he takes out his cellphone and snaps a few pictures. "Not sure we'll still be in town on Tuesday, but we'll see."

He looks around the room again. "Interesting, very interesting," he repeats, then shrugs. "Okay, let's go Moonpie."

After the two men leave, Daisy locks the door behind them. As she walks through the room towards her small apartment in the rear of the house, she passes a large mask set off from the rest. It's the face of an old man with ruddy cheeks and a full beard carved from wood, a golden crown on top of his head.

"No longer around?"

"Yeah, well, it's not a complete lie," she replies. "I don't trust that man. He's up to no good." She takes the mask off the wall and resumes walking to her quarters. "I need company tonight. I don't want to eat alone."

"Okay," the voice from the mask replies. "But after dinner, I think it would be best if you return me to the museum for the next few days...just to be on the safe side."

"Look at these prices!" Isaac exclaims, pointing to the cellphone.

"Mumph...mumph," Moonpie replies, nodding his head enthusiastically, his mouth full of spaghetti. The two men sit in a corner booth of an all-night diner a few blocks from the Mask Museum. Moonpie twirls another large ball of the pasta onto his fork and prepares to stuff his mouth again.

"That broad is sitting on a fortune, and she doesn't have a clue. Instead, she spends her time collecting a few bucks in donations from stupid tourists that stumble upon her place."

Moonpie picks up his glass of water and drains half of it before replying. "Well, maybe we should tell her so she could, I don't know, maybe sell off a few of the masks she's not crazy about."

Isaac stares at his companion like he's never heard such a stupid comment, though, in truth, he's grown accustomed to such statements from Moonpie. "No, you idiot, we're not going to tell her squat. The less she knows about what she has the better our chances. No, we have a grand opportunity here before us, and I, for one, plan to take full advantage of it."

"How's that?"

"Well, simple, really. We're going to relieve her from the burden of having to open her stupid museum ever again."

Moonpie wipes the spaghetti sauce from his mouth with the sleeve of his sweatshirt, the perpetual look of confusion growing more intense. "Really? How are we going to do that?"

"By stealing the damn masks, of course. We can sell them on the black market. In no time, we'll be rolling in the dough."

"Ahhh, I don't know, Isaac," Moonpie says, frowning. "I kinda like the ol' broad. She reminds me of my mom, rest her soul."

"Of course she does. Every old woman we've ever met reminds you of your mom. Why should this one be any different?"

"I don't know, why should she?" Moonpie squints his face in deep thought as he tries to puzzle out the answer.

"I was being sarcastic, you doofus."

"You were? About what?"

"Never mind," Isaac replies angrily. "Shut up for a few minutes while I plan this heist out."

Moonpie nods and goes back to devouring the plate of spaghetti.

The following evening, a black van pulls up and parks across the street from the Mask Museum. As Isaac turns off the engine and douses the lights, Moonpie, sitting on the passenger side, finishes off his third moon pie, wiping away the crumbs with his sleeve.

"Do we have to do this, Isaac? She's a nice lady and she really likes those masks she and her husband collected. Why don't we just go to a movie or something?"

"Aren't any movies showing in this podunk town, especially not at two in the morning," Isaac replies. "Besides, this is our big chance to make some real money, not the penny ante stuff we've been doing just to scrape by."

"But I like that stuff," Moonpie whines, then changes tactics. "I'll just stay here. You don't need me for anything."

"Oh, no, you don't. We're a team," Isaac counters. "Besides, together we can haul twice as much stuff and then get the hell out of Dodge."

"But we're in Foster Flat," Moonpie replies.

"I know where we are. It's just an expression. Oh, never mind. Come on. Grab a couple of those burlap bags while you're at it."

Isaac opens his door and climbs out, then waits until Moonpie finally follows suit. "Now, no more talking once we start. If you have to say anything at all, just whisper. I checked around and confirmed that the old lady still lives in the back rooms."

Moonpie nods as he makes a motion as though zipping his lips shut. The two men stroll across the street and up the few steps to the entrance of the museum where Isaac quickly smashes the single bulb. He then reaches into his pocket and pulls out a small flashlight and turns it on, directing the light to the window of the door.

"Break it," he orders Moonpie, who hesitates before reluctantly nodding. As he approaches the door, he takes his left hand and wraps it up in the sleeve of his sweatshirt before slamming it through the window. The crashing of the glass echoes through the night and the two men hold their breath, listening for any sound of movement from inside the house. When none is heard, Isaac reaches through the window and unlocks the door.

"Piece of cake," he mutters. He pushes the door open and walks inside as Moonpie pulls a flashlight out of his pocket, turns it on and flashes it into Isaac's eyes.

"What did you say, boss?" he asks in his normal voice, then, realizing how loud it sounds, repeats the closed zipper motion.

Isaac knocks the beam of light away. "Shut up, you fool," he hisses. He shines his own light along the walls filled with masks. They're even more macabre in the shadows of the night than before.

"Ohh, this doesn't feel good," Moonpie says. At least this time he remembers to whisper. Isaac glances at him, noticing that his partner's face has grown paler than usual.

"Don't worry about it," he tries to assure Moonpie. "They're just carved pieces of wood. Nothing to worry about. Give me one of those bags, then start filling the other one with the masks, starting over there." He points to the other end of the room. "I'll start at this end."

The two men proceed with their work, but as Isaac begins to pull a mask off the wall, he begins to feel queasy. As his hand touches the mask, it seems like the eyes have suddenly flitted to stare at him. The next moment, he sees a flash of images before him, each one a different brutal murder. He drops the mask, which clatters to the floor.

"What's up, boss?" Moonpie whispers from the other end of the room. "You okay?"

"Yeah, yeah," Isaac replies, momentarily flustered. "It just slipped out of my hand." He reaches for another mask that looks like a cross between a man and some unholy beast of prey. This time, he sees flashes of a little old lady brutally torturing dogs and cats throughout her neighborhood—a neighborhood that looks suspiciously like the one surrounding the museum. Once again, he drops the mask to the floor, but horrible images continue to fill Isaac's mind even though he's no longer touching any of the masks. Scenes from the gas chambers of Auschwitz mingle with images of a field of mass graves filled with hundreds of malnourished bodies. Then the images disappear and he's back in the room staring at the mask as it rocks back and forth on the floor. As he reaches down for it, he notices a dozen or more tarantula-size spiders clinging to his arm. He hates spiders of any size. He swats at them with his other hand.

What the fuck is going on here? he wonders, but even as he's having the thought, he feels himself running mindlessly away from the threat...until he slams into the far wall only a few feet from Moonpie, who's continuing to place masks into his sack. It's the last image Isaac sees before passing out.

As Isaac slowly awakens, he feels the top of his head threatening to lift off from the rest of his body. *Shit, I must have really tied one on last night,* he thinks. He starts to roll over before realizing he's not lying in bed. In fact, he's not lying at all, but is instead seated in a straight back chair. From the stiffness in his back and neck, he surmises he must have been in the chair for quite some time. So, how come he didn't fall out of it sometime while he slept? In the next instant, he has his answer as he tries to reach up to scratch his nose but can't. He tries with the other hand, with the same result. Finally, he opens his eyes, but then quickly shuts them again. Too bright! Way too bright. But even in that brief moment, his surroundings are imprinted on his mind, and memories of the previous night rush forth.

He's still in the Mask Museum and something is wrong—very wrong. Had that been the little old lady he'd seen across the room? And what was Moonpie doing sitting on the floor with his legs splayed out in front of him, his body held up by the wall against which he leaned? Slowly, he flutters his eyes open again, keeping his head down to minimize the amount of light that assaults them. Even so, the pounding in his head increases and he winces with pain. *Hold it together,* he tells himself. He's been in worse situations than this, although at the moment, he can't recall any quite this bad.

Finally, after several failed attempts, he manages to keep his eyes open and looks around. Everything is pretty much as it was during that first quick glance. The old woman is still standing across the room. She reaches into one of the sacks, pulls out a mask and returns it to the wall, then reaches into the sack for the next one. She's humming a little tune Isaac doesn't recognize. It's like it's just another day at the museum and a new shipment of masks has arrived, but Isaac knows better. It's got to be the next day, given the amount of sunlight streaming in from the window. He glances down at his body to confirm that, indeed, he's been tied securely to the chair, but how was that possible? Surely that old woman couldn't have lifted him into the chair. *Focus, boy,* he tells himself. *How you got in this chair is the least of your worries. How are you going to get out? Now, that's a much more important matter at the moment. But that's why I have a partner,* he argues back at himself. *Dumb as a kite but still useful in matters like this. I'll just get Moonpie to untie me.*

He stares at Moonpie where he's lying propped up against the wall not far from where the old lady continues her work. He motions with his head for Moonpie to come to him, but is only rewarded with another wave of pain, this time moving down his neck to his shoulders and beyond. The look on Moonpie's face is more vacuous than usual and the smile plastered on his lips could only be described as shit-eating. Okay, maybe his partner isn't going to be all that helpful. Let's just try a more direct approach.

"Hello there," Isaac says, but the words come out as a guttural whisper, so he tries again. "Excuse me, ma'am, there appears to have been a terrible misunderstanding here. Could you please come over here and untie me?"

The woman finishes placing one of the masks on the wall before slowly turning in his direction. "Name isn't ma'am. It's Daisy or, in your case, Mrs. Davis, and ain't no misunderstanding. You and your friend tried to steal my masks, and now you've got to pay just like any other evil person who's been caught." As she talks, she reaches down, grabs the sack and begins to drag it over to him. "Let's just see if we can't find you a proper fit." She plunks the sack down next to the chair and pulls out one of the masks, holds it up towards his face, then shakes her head. "Nope, not that one." She places it down beside the sack and picks another one from the bag, repeating the motion. The mask is pure white and reminds Isaac of a human skull. "Now, that's closer, but...not quite right."

"What the hell are you doing?" Isaac blurts out, as he struggles to free himself from the ropes around him. But whoever tied him to the chair knew what they were doing. If anything, the ropes only tighten more.

"Why, I'm finding you the right mask," Daisy replies, as though it were the most natural thing in the world. She might as well have been trying on different coats to see which one fit best. "After all, you're going to spend the rest of your existence in it. You want it to be a good fit, don't you?"

"You're crazy as a loon," Isaac spits out. "Let me go, you hear? Moonpie, you idiot, get up from there and help me," he shouts, realizing that any hope of holding it together is long gone.

"Oh, he's not really available right now," Daisy replies as she puts down the mask and reaches into the sack for a third one. "My husband...well, he needed to borrow your friend's body for a bit. Don't worry, though, he'll give it back when this nasty work is done."

"Your husband? But you said he wasn't around anymore."

"Yeah, well, he isn't, not really. You see, he died a few years back, but we had an agreement. Whichever one went first, the other one was to make sure the spirit of the dearly departed would be preserved in a mask. We even picked out the masks we'd want." She points to a large mask resembling an African chieftain that leans against the far wall not far from Moonpie. "That's my husband's over there. Once we're done with you, he'll return to it."

"What do you mean, 'done with me'?"

"Well, your body, of course," Daisy replies. "Can't have any evidence left around, you know. But don't worry, we have a nice spot picked out right next to Mrs. Curry. Now, there was a nasty lady. Worst neighbor ever. Everyone hated her and for good reason. She was a serial pet killer, but she got her due, just like you will."

Isaac remembers the flashes of horrific scenes from the night before, and it all starts to make sense in a weird, surrealistic way. "You killed your own neighbor, didn't you?"

"Sure did, and proud of it," Daisy replies. "That's been my husband and my mission for going on thirty years. We started collecting masks simply because we liked them, but then we discovered that the myths about them weren't myths at all. We realized we could do our part to collect more than masks. We've collected some of the evilest folks God ever put on this planet. And, in just a little bit, you'll get to see them. You'll fit right in with our little band of troublemakers. There's Josef Mengele and Vladimir Katriuk, both nasty Nazi murderers. Then there's Stoneman. That's not his real name, but that's what the police called him. The report was that he'd murdered thirteen people in India, but he really murdered quite a few more. The police never found him, but we did. But don't worry. We've quite a few women in our little family as well. There's Griselda Blanco. You may have read about her, though she was often referred to as the Black Widow or the Cocaine Godmother. She was a Colombian drug lord, but I think she and Stoneman may have something going right now. I'm pretty sure Mrs. Curry is unattached though."

"Moonpie!" Isaac shouts. "Get your ass up here and help me!"

Daisy reaches over with the mask she holds in her hand and raps him on the head with it. "Settle down. I told you my husband is using him at the moment. Wasn't all that hard. His simple mind was easy to circumvent. While he was at it, Reginald—that's my husband—checked out your friend's memories. It's all there. Years of you and him getting over on people, taking advantage of them, breaking the law whenever and wherever it served you. Oh, you're not of the same caliber as some of our elite criminals, but you'll do. Of course, maybe your worst offense was how you corrupted that poor boy over there. He really has a good heart, even if he is a bit simple, but once again, you used him for your own selfish purposes. That's why I think it's particularly befitting that we use him to help us end your reign of evil."

She holds up a fourth mask and gazes at it, then at Isaac. "Yep, this is the one. No doubt about it. Now, you just hold still a moment and we'll just...place...this...", but as she approaches Isaac with the mask, he begins to kick and scream, forcing Daisy to step back, shaking her head. "I was afraid you'd be one of those, but no problem." She turns around in Moonpie's direction. "Reginald, my dear, if you will assist me."

Moonpie nods and with the same moronic smile on his face, slowly stands up and lumbers over to her. "Just hold his head as steady as you can. It'll only take a minute or so for the spirit transference to take place. Then, you can haul the body down to the cellar while I tidy up here."

Moonpie nods, but then hesitates, a frown replacing the smile for just a few seconds. His body shakes as though in the throes of a struggle. For a moment, the old Moonpie takes over. "Sorry, Boss," he slurs, but then Reginald takes back control. "Oops, sorry about that, dear. He slipped out of my grasp for just a second." Moonpie proceeds to grasp Isaac's head firmly in his large mitts and holds it still as Daisy puts on the mask that resembles a human skull, but with horns on its head and a forked tongue sticking out of its mouth.

"Perfect," Daisy replies a minute or two later, removing the mask from the motionless body. She glances at her wristwatch. "Go ahead and take the body down to the cellar. Once you're through with Moonpie, clear his memory and set him out on the back porch. I'll come out with your mask."

"Can't I keep his body for just a little longer?" Reginald asks. "I've missed having the mobility."

"No," Daisy answers. "He's a good boy who's already spent too much of his life under another's thumb. It's time he got on with living without such bad influences. Besides, who'll keep the rest of our troublemakers in line if you aren't there to supervise?"

Moonpie nods. He picks up Isaac, who's still tied to the chair and carries him away. Daisy resumes her task of putting the rest of the masks on the wall, including the one with Isaac's spirit, humming quietly as she does so.

FORTUNE COOKIE
FUTURES

Master Lin Shu stared at his most loyal customer, Alfred Peterman. Not only had the man placed large orders for his family every Friday night for over five years, he'd also referred dozens of other customers to Lin Shu's Chinese Pagoda Restaurant as well.

"Listen, Lin Shu, I know I have no business asking such a favor of you, but, well, I'm desperate. If I don't find Wilbur a summer job immediately, I'll be sleeping outside with Rufus, my dog. Wilbur is my wife's favorite nephew. There have been some troubles at home, so she's agreed to take him, but it's only for the summer. After that, he'll be back home and out of my hair. Please, help me out, will you?"

Alfred grabbed a handful of business cards from the counter separating the two men. Alfred towered over Lin Shu by close to a foot, and Lin Shu figured the man weighed a good seventy-five more pounds. Not that he was all that worried that Alfred would take to violence. He had the reputation of being a quiet, peaceful man, but you never knew these days. The papers were filled with people going "postal" with a lot less provocation.

"I really don't need more help, Mr. Peterman..." Lin Shu started. As he spoke, he watched the man's face begin to collapse into a heavy look of disappointment. "But maybe I can find something for him. It'll have to be in the back, though, at least at first. Washing dishes, something like that."

"That's fine. No, really. That's more than fine. That's great," Alfred replied as he stuck the cards in his coat pocket and patted it. "I'll send everyone I meet to you. There'll be so many extra dishes to wash from the new customers, you'll have to hire a second dishwasher." He stuck out his massive hand towards Lin Shu, who took it hesitantly. He braced himself in preparation to having his hand crushed, but the large man had a surprisingly gentle handshake.

Alfred turned to leave with a renewed spring in his step and a broad smile on his face. As he began to open the door, he turned, the smile wavering a bit. "Oh, I need to let you know one thing about Wilbur. He's not the brightest light in the sky, if you get my drift." He quickly added, "But he's strong as an ox and a good worker. He won't give you any trouble, promise."

Before Lin Shu could say anything, Alfred was out the door. "What have I gotten myself into this time?" Lin Shu muttered under his breath.

But, as it turned out, Alfred was a man of his word. Not only did a steady stream of new customers start pouring through the front door carrying a business card with AP initials on the back, most of them placed large orders to compete with Alfred's, and Wilbur turned out to be a willing worker as well. Like his uncle, Wilbur was large for his sixteen years, easily six feet tall, with a layer of fat that only partially hid his muscular build. The only thing that Alfred got wrong was that his nephew was more than just a little slow. In fact, Lin Shu suspected that Wilbur suffered from some undiagnosed learning disorder, but how smart did you have to be to wash dishes and take out the trash? It seemed to Lin Shu it was a match made in heaven. And it would have been if not for his child, fifteen-year-old daughter, Lin Li and his assistant, Yang Shing.

WILBUR COULDN'T BELIEVE that Uncle Alfred had once again come through. Not only did he have a place to stay for the summer out from under his mom's tyrannical rule, but his uncle had even found him a job. Okay, maybe it wasn't the best job in the world, but it was a job that even paid. Minimum wage, but still. When he asked Uncle Alfred what he was supposed to do with his paychecks, Alfred replied, "Why, turn it over to me, of course, to pay for your room and board." Then he'd smiled. "I'm just kidding, Wilbur. It's your money. You're working for it, and you deserve it. You might want to send a little of it home to your mom, but that's completely up to you."

The suggestion made sense to Wilbur. Despite how hard his mom often was on him, he still loved her and knew, somewhere deep down inside, she loved him as well. They just needed a break from each other every now and then.

Truth be told, Wilbur enjoyed washing dishes. The hot, sudsy water made his hands feel good. He even enjoyed hauling in the supplies once or twice a week. Some of the crates were pretty heavy, but Wilbur didn't mind. It was like working out at the gym and getting paid for it. Plus, every now and then, it gave him the chance to show off to Lin Li. As far as Wilbur was concerned, Lin Li was about the prettiest girl he'd ever seen. Since she worked the register up front and was seldom around the food preparation, she wore her long, jet black hair down. She had large, expressive, dark brown, almond-shaped eyes and a quirky smile with just the slightest sign of dimples on both cheeks just below the high cheekbones. Her porcelain skin was so smooth it made you want to reach out and caress her cheek—not that Wilbur would ever do such a thing. No, he was terrified of girls. All girls, but especially beautiful ones. He'd have to settle for admiring Lin Li from afar.

THEN THERE WAS YANG Shing, the assistant manager of the Pagoda—at least that's the title he had used when he'd introduced himself on that first day. Despite being at least a year or two older than Wilbur, Shing was almost a foot shorter, but he seemed determined to make up for his small frame by being meaner than anyone else Wilbur had ever met. When he'd mention this to his uncle, he'd frowned and replied, "Sounds like a classic case of Napoleon Syndrome."

"What's that?" Wilbur asked with a perplexed look on his face—the same look that he often wore.

"Small people, especially men, sometimes feel the need to compensate for their small size in some way. I'd stay clear of him if you can. Just do what he says and don't cause waves. It wasn't easy getting you that job. There aren't that many opportunities here in Foster Flat for teenagers, but a ton of kids looking for work."

Wilbur tried his darnedest to follow his uncle's advice but, given the small size of the restaurant, it was nearly impossible to stay out of Shing's way. In fact, it felt like Shing went out of his way to get in Wilbur's face, especially since that first episode shortly after Wilbur started working there. Lin Shu had called the other workers to the back of the restaurant to introduce their newest employee. The two cooks simply shook Wilbur's hand before returning to the kitchen to prepare for the onslaught of lunchtime customers, leaving Shu to introduce his daughter, Lin Li, and his assistant, Yang Shing.

"Assistant manager, that is," Shing corrected his boss, while also ignoring Wilbur's offered hand. "I'll be keeping a close eye on you, boy, so do your work and no fraternizing with the customers or the other employees. Understand?"

Wilbur nodded, even though he hadn't a clue what it meant to 'fraternize.' He figured he'd just stay to himself until he could ask his uncle what it meant.

"It's a pleasure to meet you, Wilbur," Lin Li said as she took the hand he'd offered to Shing. Wilbur turned to reply to her greeting, but found that his tongue had suddenly grown four sizes larger and had forgotten how to form words, much less a coherent sentence. He nodded to her, continuing to hold her hand for several seconds as he stared into her eyes.

"Okay, everyone, back to work," Lin Shu said as he quietly took his daughter's hand from Wilbur's large mitt. "Lunchtime will be upon us before we know it." He continued to hold his daughter's hand as he escorted her to the front of the restaurant.

"Already breaking my one order, huh?" Shing said after the two of them left. He took a set of sticks out of his back pocket and started swinging them around so fast that Wilbur had trouble focusing on them. "Ever seen a set of these?" Shing asked, pausing just long enough for Wilbur to see that the two sticks were painted a dull red and were connected together somehow. Then he twirled them around his body again as Wilbur shook his head and instinctively took a step away from him.

"They're nunchaku, or as most Americans call them, nunchucks," Shing continued. "What did I tell you about fraternizing with the customers and other employees?"

"You said not to do it," Wilbur replied as he continued to stare at the twirling sticks, mesmerized by the rapid motion, while at the same time being frightened that Shing might lose control and conk one or both of them on the head.

"And yet, already you start flirting with Lin Li...in front of me, no less."

"I wasn't...I didn't..." Wilbur stuttered, unsure what he was trying to say. All thought stopped when suddenly Shing turned his attention to a large burlap bag of rice sitting a few feet from Wilbur. The nunchuck flew through the air at blinding speed, landing with a solid dull thump on the bag of rice...once...twice...a third time, all faster than Wilbur could follow. Shing continued to beat on the bag until the burlap suddenly split and grains of rice fell to the floor.

"Lin Li is already spoken for," Shing said as he turned his attention back to Wilbur. "Understand, boy?"

Wilbur nodded, too alarmed by the violence exercised on the innocent bag of rice to say anything.

"I believe the words you're looking for are, 'yes sir,'" Shing said as he returned the nunchucks to his back pocket.

"Yes, sir," Wilbur replied.

"Now clean this shit up." Shing turned to leave, then stopped. "And don't forget this lesson."

WILBUR SPENT MOST OF his time in the rear of the restaurant with his hands in hot soapy water, scrubbing pots and pan as well as endless stacks of dirty dishes. He really didn't mind though, for as he worked, he also enjoyed creating stories in which he was the hero regularly rescuing Lin Li from one dangerous mishap after another. But occasionally he was allowed to come to the front after hours when the doors had been locked and all the customers had left for the evening. After all, someone had to clean the floors in preparation for the next day.

That's where Wilbur discovered the magic powers of fortune cookies from, of all people, Yang Shing. One night not long after Wilbur had started work, Shing sat up front in one of the booths deciding what specials to offer the next day. Watching Wilbur as he swept the floor in preparation for mopping it, he had a sudden brainstorm.

Shing reached into the large tub of fortune cookies and pulled out two, opening one for himself before looking over to Wilbur.

"Hey, boy, you like cookies? Ever tried one of these?" he asked as he tossed the second cookie at Wilbur, who instinctively caught it.

"Yeah, I love them," Wilbur replied, staring down at the cellophane-wrapped cookie.

"Well, then you'll like these, too." Shing broke off a piece of his own cookie and popped it in his mouth. "Try it."

It took Wilbur several seconds to figure out how to remove the cellophane. His large hands often made such detail work difficult, but when he, at last, had it removed, he popped the whole cookie in his mouth.

"What are you doing, you idiot?" Shing started to say, but stopped himself at the last second. *Let him figure it out*, he thought, smiling while Wilbur crunched on the cookie. A second or two later, he stopped, that familiar, perplexed look growing on his face as he reached into his mouth with two beefy fingers and pulled out a slip of paper.

"What's this?"

"It's your fortune, dunderhead. Haven't you ever heard of a fortune cookie?"

Wilbur shook his head as he started chewing on the cookie again. "No, but they're good."

"Well, aren't you going to read your fortune?" Shing asked after a few seconds. "You can read, can't you?"

"Sure," Wilbur replied. Reading was one of his favorite pastimes, but something told him not to share this fact with Shing. Instead, he looked at the paper and slowly read the words:

"You will be visited by old friends before the end of the month."

"That's a good one," Shing said as he prepared the next step of his plan. "I hope, for your sake, you have some old friends. If so, you might want to call a few and make sure someone comes to visit you soon. The end of the month is only a week away. Wouldn't want to anger the gods, you know."

"What?" Wilbur didn't like the ominous sound of Shing's comment. "What gods?"

"The fortune cookie gods, of course. They are easily angered if their fortunes are ignored. So, even if you need to help them come true, it's far better than what can happen if they don't come true."

"Really?" Wilbur finished swallowing the last morsel of the cookie. Suddenly, he wasn't sure he liked it that much after all. "Well, my mom is supposed to come for a visit this weekend. Will that count?"

"I don't know," Shing said, suppressing the grin that fought to spread across his face. "Do you consider her a friend?"

Wilbur thought about that for a moment before answering. After all, the gods might be listening. Finally, he replied, "Yeah, sure. We're friends...most of the time."

"Well, then, you're off the hook," Shing replied, allowing a little smile to surface. "This time."

OVER THE NEXT COUPLE weeks, Yang Shing continued to feed additional fortune cookies to his new mark. The only difference was that these cookies had special fortunes that Shing wrote especially for Wilbur. Shing considered it an experiment to see just how gullible Wilbur was and how far he'd go to avoid the wrath of the fortune cookie gods. It also seemed like an ideal way to make sure Wilbur and Lin Li didn't hook up. He had to admit that, like most experiments, this one had mixed results.

Wilbur's next fortune read: "Tell your beloved how you really feel about her." Shing figured that would turn Lin Li off in a heartbeat, not to mention how her father would blow a gasket when he heard about it. Unfortunately, it didn't unfold in quite the way he'd planned.

"Well, what are you going to do?" Shing asked as he watched Wilbur mull over the fortune while he munched on the cookie. "Remember, those gods don't like to be ignored."

"Yeah, I know," Wilbur replied. "I'm thinking, I'm thinking."

"I wouldn't think too long," Shing prodded him as he cracked open his own cookie and pretended to read what was inside. "Oh, my. Listen to this: 'Help your friend strike while the iron is hot.' If that's not a sign, I don't know what is. I think I saw Lin Li in her father's office working on the books."

Wilbur nodded. "Can I take a couple of minutes and..."

"Sure, no problem. I don't want the gods mad at me either. Take however much time you need."

Wilbur nodded again, then lumbered towards the rear of the building. Shing waited for a few seconds before following behind him. *This is going to be too good to miss*, he thought. He watched as Wilbur entered the small closet-size room that Lin Shu had converted to an office. Shing peered around the corner as Wilbur shuffled in front of the desk where Lin Li sat. He spoke to her for a few moments but Shing was too far away to make out his words. After another moment, Wilbur picked up the phone from the desk and started dialing a number.

What the hell is he doing? Shing wondered. *Who would he be calling now while his beloved sits right there in front of him?* After a couple of minutes, Wilbur hung up the phone and spoke again to Lin Li. The next moment froze Shing in his tracks as Lin Li rose from her seat behind the desk and walked around to give dunderhead Wilbur a hug.

This can't be, Shing thought. *He wasn't even talking to her.* He had to find out what was going on, so he could somehow fix it. After Wilbur left to go back to his dishwashing duties, Shing sauntered forward.

"What was that all about?" he asked, pointing in the direction Wilbur had just gone. "What did he want?"

Lin Li looked up from the papers she'd started working on again and smiled. "It was the sweetest thing. He just came in to ask if he could use the phone for a minute. Then he called his mother just to tell her how much he loved her. What a sweetie pie."

"You've got to be kidding. His mother?"

"That's right. My father has always told me to be sure to check to see how a boy treats his mother because it's a good sign of how he'll treat you. I think he's right."

"Son-of-a-bitch," Shing muttered as he turned to leave.

"When was the last time you called your mother?" Lin Li asked. "Oh, never mind. I forgot. You still live with her."

THE NEXT PHASE OF THE experiment started out better. Late one evening as Wilbur finished the mopping, Shing pretended to pull a cookie from the bin, then handed the one he had hidden in his palm to Wilbur. The fortune cookie read: "Tomorrow is a bad day to work. Stay home."

"Oh, that doesn't sound good," Wilbur said as he stared at the paper.

"No, indeed, it does not," Shing replied. "I think the fortune cookie gods may be testing you."

"Testing me?" Wilbur asked, as he absentmindedly tossed a chunk of cookie into his mouth.

"Yeah, they want to know if you'll do what it takes to stay on their good side. But this is a good thing, really. It's your opportunity to show them how much you trust their guidance. I've heard that once someone passes such a test, the gods often bring them their heart's desire. Wouldn't that be cool?"

"For sure," Wilbur replied, as his gaze drifted off.

"Get your dirty mind off my girl," Shing started to shout, but said instead, "So, what are you going to do?"

Wilbur thought a moment before replying, "I guess I'll call Lin Shu and ask if I can have tomorrow off."

"You're going to call him this late?" Shing said. "Really? He hates being called at home, especially about something that's going to mess his schedule up the next day. Maybe you better let me take care of it for you."

"You'd do that for me?" Wilbur asked.

"Well, only because it involves the gods," Shing replied. "It's not smart to mess with them."

"I really appreciate it." Wilbur hesitated for a moment before walking over and giving Shing a hug. " I don't know how to repay you."

"Maybe you can put a good word in for me with the gods," Shing said, as he felt his ribs start to crack. *This dude is strong as an ox and twice as stupid*, he thought. He almost felt sorry for him. Almost.

The next morning when Lin Shu entered his office, Shing was already there. "We have a problem," he said, frowning as though he'd just lost his best friend.

"Good morning to you too, Shing. Can't you at least wait until I get my second cup of tea before dropping bad news on me?"

"I'm sorry, but it's not of my doing," Shing replied. "It's Wilbur. He won't be in today. We'll have to find someone else to wash the dishes and take out the trash."

"Really? That's curious. He's been so dependable," Lin Shu replied. "How did this come about?"

"I don't know for sure. He just told me late last night that he had other plans for today. I tried to get more out of him, even explained what a hardship it would cause, but to no avail. He just said he really needed a break. You know, you just can't get good help these days. These kids..."

"Now wait just a minute. Don't go berating our kids. We've had good fortune with those we've employed and that includes Wilbur. I wasn't all that keen on the idea when his uncle first approached me, but he's been a godsend. I think he's right. He does deserve a day off. I really don't see a problem here at all."

"You don't?" Shing asked. "But who'll wash the dishes, take out the trash? And there's a shipment of supplies due in this afternoon. Who's going to take care of that?"

"Why, that's what I have an assistant manager for," Lin Shu replied. "I'm sure you'll handle it all. I'll give Wilbur a call later today and make sure everything is okay with his family."

"But...but," Shing stuttered.

"I think you had better get to it. Speaking of trash, it looks like that darn raccoon came back last night. How about going out there and cleaning up the mess he made. Wouldn't want our neighboring businesses to complain, now would we?"

BY THE END OF THE DAY—A day filled to overflowing with dirty dishes, trash that had been trashed by the local wildlife, and carrying crates and bags of supplies that weighed almost as much as he did—Shing decided to end the experiment. He upgraded it to a full fledged vendetta against Wilbur.

Shing recalled a classmate of his once trying to enroll him into playing a computer game where the main character was a mythological god by the name of Ling Tian. While Shing found the game to be silly, as he found most such games, he did become fascinated with the god. According to Chinese legend, Ling Tian had fought against the Supreme Divinity, only to have apparently lost the battle and been beheaded. But not so fast. Even though his head was buried in some distant mountain, Ling Tian persevered, his nipples turning into eyes and his belly button becoming a mouth. It was time for Shing to persevere as well.

Somehow he needed to discredit Wilbur, not only in the eyes of Lin Li but also in her father's eyes. In fact, why not shame him so severely that news would spread all over town? Shing knew what a powerful rumor and gossip mill Foster Flat possessed. He just needed to come up with some elegant plan that would ruin Wilbur's reputation, maybe even the reputation of his aunt and uncle while he was at it. Drive the whole pack of them out of town. Yeah, that was the goal. Now, he just needed a plan.

It came to him in an unusual way, as his most ingenious plans often did. He was standing in the checkout line in his neighborhood Fast Mart, fuming that he had to wait while several people in front of him bought lottery tickets. As he studied them, he realized that they all had one thing in common, not only with each other, but with Wilbur as well. They were all losers. When it was finally his turn to check out, he smiled at the old man behind the register.

"You have a lot of people buying tickets today, don't you?" he asked noncommittally.

"Yeah, today and every other day," the wizened old man replied, shaking his head and frowning. "Don't they know they've almost no chance of winning. Better to just throw their money away."

"Or give it to you or me," Shing replied.

The man chuckled. "There you go." He gave Shing his change. "To me, it's the height of irresponsibility as they try to take the easy way to riches and it never pans out, not only for the person, but also for their loved ones. What a waste of time. I told my daughter when she was old enough to start dating, find out if your beau likes to buy lottery tickets. If he does, run the other way. For once in her life, she took my advice. She's now married to a hardworking man who's never bought a lottery ticket in his life, and she's happier for it."

That's it! Shing thought, as he strolled out of the store and to his car. The old man had sounded just like Lin Shu, who also held hard work as an important virtue. He just needed to persuade Wilbur to buy some lottery tickets and make sure Lin Li and her father found out about it. *This will be a piece of cake*, Shing thought. Fortune cookies already had lottery ticket numbers printed on them. Shing whistled all the way back to work. It had turned into a very good day. Tomorrow would be even better.

That evening Shing made it a point to stay late even though several customers refused to leave at closing, making it even later before they could finally lock the doors. He assured Lin Shu that he'd stay until everything was set for the next day, then sent him home. A short time later, Wilbur appeared with mop and bucket in hand. Shing nodded at him but then returned to the order forms he was pretending to work on. Finally, when Wilbur was close to finishing mopping the floor, Shing stood up, stretched, and walked over to the bin of fortune cookies. He picked up one for himself and added it to the one in his palm, being careful not to get them mixed up.

He tossed the doctored up cookie to Wilbur, who caught it, but then just stared at it without opening it.

"What's the matter?" Shing asked as he opened his and broke off a piece. "Aren't you hungry?"

"It's not that," Wilbur replied. "I've just been thinking. If I don't open the cookie, I won't have to worry about offending the gods. While I enjoy eating them, it seems like there's a risk that comes with it. I'm not sure it's worth it."

"Ahh, I see," Shing replied, momentarily puzzled by Wilbur's response. "Just one thing wrong with your thinking, Wilbur, my boy. You've already accepted the fortune cookie as soon as you caught it. Failing to open it to read the fortune is the ultimate offense. Everyone knows that."

Wilbur gulped, a worried look growing on his face. "Well, I didn't."

"Tch, tch. You know what they say, 'ignorance of the law is no excuse.' Ignorance of these mystical laws of the fortune cookie included. Besides, what do you have to worry about? Everything has turned out well for you so far, hasn't it?"

"Yeah, I guess," Wilbur replied, though he didn't sound convinced.

"That cookie might just have the best fortune ever right inside that delectable cookie, and besides, I'm right here to help you if you need it."

"Well, okay," Wilbur finally said. He stripped off the cellophane and cracked the cookie in half to reveal the slip of paper inside. "Here goes." He sighed heavily and read what was on the paper. "Amazing fortune is on its way with these lottery numbers."

He glanced up from the paper to meet Shing's gaze. "That's a weird one. What does it mean?"

Shing returned Wilbur's stare with a straight face. *Like shooting fish in a barrel*, he thought. "Sounds to me like the gods are asking you to trust them enough to play the lottery. You do know what the lottery is, don't you?"

"Yeah, kinda," Wilbur replied, "but I've never played it. I'm not sure I'd know how."

"It's easy. See those numbers on the back of the paper? Every fortune has them."

"Yeah, I was wondering what those were for."

They're for fools like you, my idiot child, Shing thought. "Those are the numbers you use. Just take them into any place where they sell lottery tickets. Give them those numbers."

"That's simple enough."

Yeah, even an idiot like you can't screw it up. Shing smiled. "Easy, peasy." Then he frowned.

"What? What's wrong?" Wilbur asked, noticing the change in his Shing's expression.

"What happens if you don't win?"

"Oh, yeah. That would be bad, wouldn't it?"

"The worst." Shing pretended to mull this over, chewing on his lower lip before finally adding, "The more tickets you buy, the better your odds of winning."

"O...kay," Wilbur replied. He thought about it for a minute more. "Well, I did get my paycheck today."

"Perfect! And the big drawing is tomorrow evening, so by Sunday you could be rolling in the dough," Shing exclaimed, even though he'd known all along that it was payday. It had been why he'd waited to spring his trap. "Each lottery ticket is only good for one set of numbers, but you could buy more tickets with numbers around these until your money runs out. That should do it."

Wilbur's brow crinkled as he tried to grasp this strategy. "I was planning on sending some of the money home to my mom."

"Well, it's your life," Shing answered. "Not sure the cookie gods will be all that pleased with that decision, but..." He left the thought hanging in space, waiting for Wilbur to hang himself on it.

"You're right," Wilbur finally replied. "I can always send her money next time I get paid. Or better yet, I can send her some of my winnings."

"There you go! Problem solved." At least Shing felt certain his primary problem by the name of Wilbur Peterman would soon be resolved once and for all.

Shing thought the next several hours would never pass. He could hardly wait until Sunday morning when the restaurant opened. Everyone arrived for work early on Sundays since it was one of their busiest days, so it was easy to arrange to have Lin Li and Lin Shu in the same room when Wilbur shuffled in.

"Well, how did it go?" Shing asked, trying hard not to gloat, but failing miserably.

"Okay," Wilbur replied with a slight smile on his face. "Yes, I'd say it went okay. At least I haven't had any sign that the gods are mad at me."

"What are you two talking about?" Lin Shu asked, as he paused folding napkins in the shape of swans, a trademark of the Pagoda's Sunday brunches.

"Oh, nothing," Shing replied before Wilbur had a chance to speak up. "Wilbur was just telling me the other night how he planned to spend his entire paycheck on lottery tickets. Pretty wild, isn't it? That's where part of the restaurant money went this week."

"Really?" Lin Shu replied, a frown growing on his face. "That seems rash to me."

"Father," Lin Li spoke up. "It is Wilbur's money to do with as he pleases."

"Yes, I guess you're right," her father replied. "Still..."

"Oh, don't worry, I didn't spend my paycheck that way." Wilbur turned to Shing. "I'm sorry. I know that was what you advised me to do, but after thinking about it, well, it just didn't feel right. So I kept with my original plan and sent my mom some money and I'll put the rest in the bank on Monday."

"What did you just say?" Lin Shu came around from behind the table where he'd been working and walked over to Shing. "You advised him to spend his entire paycheck on playing the lottery? What kind of advice are you giving this boy?"

"Well, I...huh, I don't know..." Shing stammered, backing away from the little man. "I might have suggested that as one possibility, but..."

He turned in Wilbur's direction. *I've got to shut this idiot up*, he thought. He pulled the nunchucks from his back pocket and showed them to Wilbur while hiding them from the Lins with his body. "Remember what happened to that sack of rice?" he whispered between clenched teeth. Wilbur shrugged and smiled.

"It's okay, Mr. Lin, really it is," Wilbur assured him. "Like I said, it all worked out. I figured this was another opportunity to trust the fortune cookie gods and see how it went."

"Fortune cookie gods? Where did you hear such a foolish..." Lin Shu stopped as he noticed Shing's face growing red and perspiration beginning to run down his face. "You?"

"I'm shocked that you would fill this boy's head with such drivel," Lin Li agreed.

Shing glanced first to Lin Shu and then to Lin Li. It had suddenly grown very hot in the restaurant and he felt like he was going to faint. He took another step towards Wilbur, spinning the nunchucks in front of him, trying to hide the motion from the Lins.

Once more Wilbur stepped in to defend him.

"It really is all right. We were just having some fun playing a game. I never really took his story about fortune cookie gods all that serious. It was just something to pass the time. Besides, turns out I really like the taste of fortune cookies." He dug into his jeans pocket and pulled out a single lottery ticket.

"I still don't know if there's a fortune cookie god or not, but if there is, he seems to like me just fine." He held the ticket up for everyone to see. "I won the big prize. I won't just be able to send money home to my mom. I'll be able to buy her a whole new home wherever she wants it."

They were the last words Shing heard clearly. As he took a final step towards Wilbur with the intention of silencing him once and for all, something happened that he would never be able to explain. The spinning path of the nunchuck altered slightly, crashing the end against his own head. As he fell to the floor like a sack of rice, he could just make out Lin Li throwing herself into Wilbur's arms. As the darkness folded over him, he thought he heard Lin Li exclaim, "I love a man who stays in good favor with the gods."

THE APOTHECARY

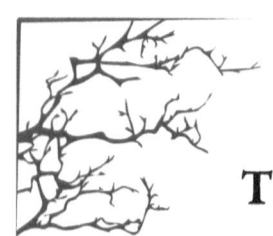

The Apothecary was teeming with energy even though it was well past lunchtime. Lunch-goers filled most of the fifteen tables and booths, many of whom were enjoying a second cup of coffee. The stools at the counter were also filled. Entering into the Apothecary was like stepping back in time to the early fifties, even for the residents of the rustic mountain town of Foster Flat. Fatima Flat, the great-granddaughter of Phineas Flat, founder of the mountain village, had meticulously restored the narrow hall-like breakfast and lunch spot. It had grown into one of the most popular hangouts for residents and likewise a not-to-miss location for tourists.

A young woman with flowing jet black hair cascading down her back stepped out of the back room with her latest patient, elderly Mrs. Elnora Primcastle, following close behind.

"Oh, Fatima, I'm feeling better already," Mrs. Primcastle said in her high-pitched voice that carried throughout the restaurant. "You're just the best." She turned to the other lunch-goers who had turned in her direction. "She's the best, I tell you. Whatever you've got that ails you, she can cure it."

Fatima turned in her direction, blushing. "It's not me, Mrs. Primcastle. As I've told you before, I'm just an assistant to the great healing powers of your own body, along with a little help from good ol' Mother Nature and her herbs.

"Be sure to put the cream I gave you on that area for the next several days, and let me know if the rash doesn't continue to clear up," Fatima continued, as she grasped the old lady's hand and gave it a gentle pat. Mrs. Primcastle strolled out of the Apothecary, stopping at several tables to again applaud Fatima's amazing abilities. Fatima smiled as she watched her leave, then turned around to prepare for her next patient.

She stopped at one of the tables, where a young girl about ten years of age sat with a scattering of papers in front of her instead of food. She was turned in her chair, chatting with a large man wearing bib overalls.

"Remember, Flower," Fatima admonished, "I said you have to stay focused on your schoolwork if you're going to insist on taking up a table during lunch. Now, leave Mr. Whimpleman alone so he can finish his meal."

"Oh, she's no..." Mr. Whimpleman started, but then noticed the stern look from Fatima and stopped. "Yeah, uh, listen to what your mother says. Back to your studies, young lady."

"Yes, Mommie Dearest," Flower replied.

Fatima waited for her to turn back in her seat, then gently caressed her daughter's hair, which was as thick and curly as her own.

"What a lovely child," Mr. Whimpleman added, "but then again, why should I be surprised? She has such a beautiful and gifted mother."

"That's enough of your blarney, you old coot. Finish your meal and get on with your day," Fatima replied, but with a lilt to her voice that suggested she enjoyed the farmer's kind words. She turned her attention from him to gaze towards the front of the building that had been such a vital part of her life ever since she was the little girl doing her homework at one of the tables. She loved this place with all of her heart, everything from the coin-operated carousel horse that still worked despite the hundreds of kids that rode it every year, to the rows and rows of antique apothecary jars lining the wall behind the lunch counter.

She shook her head. *Now who's woolgathering?* she thought. She was about to turn around again when she noticed a young, distinguished looking man standing at the front door, his deep blue eyes staring straight at her, a slight smile on his face. *Who's he?* she wondered, surprised to feel the heat returning to her cheeks. She knew everyone in town, so that must mean he was a tourist, but for some reason, he didn't seem like a tourist. Then she remembered hearing a rumor that a new physician was supposed to be relocating to the area. It had been close to five years since Dr. Plimpton had retired and moved to Florida. Since then, if you needed a doctor, you had to travel to Black Mountain, over thirty miles away. *Could this be him? If so, wouldn't that make him my competition? Don't be silly. There's plenty of room for another person dedicated to healing and helping.* She finally broke her gaze and started back to her office in the rear of the building. *So why do I suddenly feel so threatened by him?*

DR. HAROLD HARPER GAZED around the restaurant he'd heard so much about from the few townsfolk that had wandered into Plimpton's old office as he was in the process of cleaning it up. *So this is the Apothecary,* he thought, surprised to find it so full considering it was close to three o'clock, well past the regular time for lunch. His gaze fell on the bright face of a young woman standing in the middle of the room. *Is that her?* he wondered. She certainly fit the description he'd been given: long, luscious hair the color of a tunnel in midnight, a creamy texture to her complexion that suggested some Eastern influence in her lineage. He watched as she turned around and headed towards the back, stopping long enough to talk to a little girl sitting alone at one of the tables. *No one told me she had a daughter,* he thought. But the lack of any signs of another parent around was just one clue. The most obvious was that the girl looked like a mini version of her mother...with one small, yet significant difference, Harper noted, as he watched the girl close her books and start to follow her mother to the back with a noticeable limp of her left leg.

Even from this distance, he could tell that the problem was with her deformed left ankle. He'd seen several similar cases through the years while assisting at his father's orthopedic practice, but he couldn't remember seeing one quite so severe and in such a young patient. *How unfortunate,* he thought, *to have dedicated your life to helping other people with their sore throats and rashes, but be unable to help your own daughter.*

Hold on there, Hopalong, Harper berated himself. *Let's not go getting soft now, just because the woman is one of the most breathtaking beauties you've ever seen. Remember, she's your competition, and if the rumors are true, a competitor practicing medicine without a license.*

Besides, today was just a fact-finding mission. That, and an opportunity to check out the food, which he'd heard was the best lunch in town. He sat down at one of the old-timey stools at the lunch counter and ordered a club sandwich and ice tea. Twenty minutes later, he had to admit that the rumors had turned out to be true. It was the best club sandwich he'd ever eaten, its flavor enhanced by the fresh basil leaves. *That's a good thing,* he thought. *At least that way, Ms.*

Fatima Flat will still have a way to feed herself and her daughter after the State Board of Medical Examiners closes her illegal practice. As he paid for his meal, he made a mental note to call the Board as soon as he returned to his office. State Medical Boards were notoriously slow to respond to such complaints. Best go ahead and start the process so he could get on with growing his new practice. He spun around in his seat to leave, just in time to see the miniature version of Fatima limp out from the kitchen area with a clean towel in one hand and a spray bottle in the other.

"After you clean the tables, Flower, I'll take you to the park for a little bit. It's such a beautiful spring day. Hate to waste it inside," her mother called from the other room.

Flower. What a pretty name, Harper thought. *I guess it's not that surprising for a herbalist to name her daughter after a beauty of nature. Steady, man. On to the business at hand.*

"YOU LOOK TIRED, MOMMIE Dearest. We don't need to go to the playground today," Flower said, with a slight smile on her face.

Wait for it, Fatima thought. *The little snip is going to try to con me into something. Her use of Mommie Dearest is a dead giveaway.*

"Why don't you go upstairs and take a nap. I'd just as soon wait until this weekend and go with you to search for herbs."

There it is. Fatima groaned softly. Her scavenger hunts to the woods had become a sore topic of late. When Flower was still a baby, she'd been able to carry her in a sling. Later, she'd graduated to pulling Flower in a wagon, but that was getting increasingly difficult as her daughter continued to grow.

"You know how much I enjoy our outings into nature, Dearheart," Fatima said as she bent down to her daughter's level, "but I'm planning to head up to the Glassy Mountain area this week to look for some Yellowroot and Wild Bergamot. That's a challenging trek by myself. I just don't see how I'll be able to take you along this time."

Flower stuck out her lower lip and sighed heavily. "But, Mom..."

So much for Mommie Dearest.

"I really want to go." The whine in her voice tugged at Fatima's heartstrings. "This darn leg won't let me do anything." Flower kicked at her bad ankle with her good foot.

"Now, dear. Please don't do that." Fatima reached out to hug her daughter. "I'll see what I can work out. I'll ask around to see if anyone else knows where we can find the herbs."

"But you've already done that," Flower countered.

"I know, I know," Fatima replied, feeling the frustration mounting. "But for now, let's go to the playground. I'll push you on the swing."

"Oh, all right," Flower said reluctantly. "But I can swing myself. That's one thing I can do."

"Okay, dear. Whatever you say."

OVER THE NEXT WEEK, Dr. Harper found himself drawn back time and again to the Apothecary. At first, he justified it to himself that everyone needed to eat and, being a bachelor, cooking wasn't one of his many talents. *Besides, it just makes sense to keep a close eye on my competition and build evidence for when that Dr. Bastion arrives from the Board of Examiners.* He'd received a call back a couple days after filing the complaint notifying him that a Dr. Alexander Bastion had been assigned to the case and would be in touch within a week or two. *Typical bureaucratic red tape and delayed action*, he thought at the time.

But as the days flowed by and he found himself eating all his breakfasts and lunches at the Apothecary, he began to regret having made the call in the first place. The feeling grew worse after meeting Flower during lunch one day. He'd been sitting at his favorite spot at the lunch counter enjoying a second glass of iced tea, when he felt someone standing behind him. As he was about to turn around, he heard a small voice say, "I don't know you."

He spun around on the stool, but at first failed to see who had spoken to him, then glanced down to find the little girl staring at him, a look of curiosity on her face. "I know everyone who comes in here," she continued, "but I don't know you. Who are you?"

Harper smiled at her bold straightforwardness. "Why, I'm Dr. Harold Harper, at your service," he replied.

"You're a doctor? A real doctor?" Flower asked, the look of curiosity turning to one of amazement.

"That's right," Harper replied. "Recently graduated from Duke University."

"How tall are you?"

The question caught Harper by surprise. "About six foot two or thereabouts."

"And how much do you weigh?"

Harper stared at her for a second before finally replying, "I don't know, around a hundred eighty-five." *Probably closer to two hundred,* he thought, but decided a little fudging wouldn't hurt anything. "Why do you ask?"

"That's big enough," Flower replied, ignoring his question. Instead, she turned towards the back of the restaurant and yelled at the top of her voice. "Mommie Dearest, I found our answer."

A moment later, Fatima rushed out from the back. "Why in the world are you yelling? Are you okay?" She stared at the man sitting near her daughter, a suspicious look on her face that quickly changed to one of recognition. "It's you."

Harper stood up and held out his hand. "You have a lovely daughter. We were just getting acquainted. I'm Dr. Harper."

"I know who you are," Fatima replied, ignoring the extended hand. "What are you doing bothering my daughter?"

Harper opened his mouth to answer, but before he could say anything, Flower spoke up. "He's not bothering me. He's our answer."

"He's what?" Fatima turned to stare at her daughter. "What in the world are you talking about?"

"He's over six feet tall, and he says he weighs a hundred and eighty-five pounds, though he's probably closer to two hundred. He's big enough he could carry me on our trip to Glassy Mountain this weekend."

Fatima and Dr. Harper both stared at the little girl standing between them, matching looks of astonishment on their faces.

"You see, I have a bum leg," Flower continued, as she held out her left leg to show him. "But my mom needs to go up to Glassy Mountain to look for some herbs she needs. I reeeaaally want to go. It's one of the favorite things we do together, but she thinks I'm too heavy for her to carry. But you could carry me, couldn't you?" She stopped to catch her breath before finishing with, "Pleeeaaase!"

There was a long pause before Fatima's and Harper's gazes slowly moved from Flower to each other. "I'm so sorry," Fatima finally said. "I had no idea what she was planning. Please accept my apology."

"No, no," Harper replied. "No need to apologize. I find her forthrightness quite refreshing. In fact, I have no plans for this weekend. I'd be more than happy to help out. I could use some good exercise. Seems I have about fifteen pounds I need to lose."

"Oh, I don't know about that," Fatima replied, gazing up and down at him. "You seem to be...well, quite fit, I'd say." Her face flushed.

"Then, it's a date," Harper declared.

"No, it's not," Fatima objected. "It's a...it's an arrangement. I'll pay you for your services. Good day." With that, she grabbed her daughter's hand and turned on her heels, retreating to the kitchen.

FATIMA PAUSED AT THE crest of an overlook to catch her breath and appreciate the gorgeous weather and deep blue skies dotted here and there with a few puffy clouds. She took a deep breath of the clean mountain air and slowly released it. She turned slowly to watch Dr. Harper, with Flower on his back, trudging up the steep grade and smiled despite herself. Evidently, he wasn't in quite as good a shape as she'd first thought, but then, what had she expected from a city boy who'd probably spent the last several years with his nose in boring books of academia?

"Are you going to make it?" she called down to him. "We still have close to a mile before we're at the summit where we'll find the herbs."

Harper paused to adjust Flower's position on his back and looked up to her. "We're doing just fine, aren't we, Flower? We're simply taking our time to fully take in the beauty all around us."

"That's right. Now, hop to it horsey," Flower said, as she playfully pounded on one of his shoulders.

"Easy there, Missy," Fatima said with a chuckle. "You don't want to be accused of animal cruelty, now, do you?"

"No, ma'am. That's why I brought a couple apples to feed him...once we're at the top, that is."

"You remind me of my old advisor, always pushing, pushing," Harper said as he started walking again.

"Believe me, the view from the top of Glassy Mountain will be well worth the effort," Fatima said. "I just hope we find that the herbs are ready for picking."

They were not disappointed by either the view or the vegetation. Both herbs were in the prime of new growth. Fatima pulled out two paper bags and filled them with the green leaves and roots. The three of them then sat on a large boulder of granite that overlooked the valley, enjoying the turkey with basil sandwiches Fatima had made that morning.

They ate in silence for several minutes. Finally, Fatima decided now was the time to ask a question that had troubled her for the last few days. "Dr. Harper, may I ask you a question, one professional to another?"

"Sure you may, if you'll call me Harold. Dr. Harper is my dad."

"Oh, okay. I guess I can do that." She paused, suddenly unsure whether it was a good idea to bring up the subject. *Too late now,* she thought. *Go ahead. He might actually be able to help in some way.* "I received a letter a couple days ago from the Board of Medical Examiners. They're sending someone out to talk to me about my healing practice. Do I have anything to worry...about?" She hesitated, alarmed by the sudden look on Harper's face. "What? What's wrong? Am I in trouble?"

Harper stared down at his hands. Finally, he looked up at her and tried to smile. "No. Well, at least not yet, but I am."

"What are you talking about?"

"I'm afraid I'm the one who notified the Board."

"You what? Why would you do a thing like that?" Fatima shouted.

"Mommie Dearest, it'll be okay," Flower said.

Fatima glanced at her daughter, who was apparently frightened by the sudden outburst. She took a deep breath to control her anger before continuing in an only slightly calmer voice. "No, dear heart, I'm afraid it's not okay. It appears that our dear ol' doctor here can't stand a little competition, so he's taken actions to have my practice closed down."

"You did that?" Flower asked, frowning at her new friend.

"Well, I didn't know either of you at the time," Harper replied, at a loss as to what to say.

"You have no idea how many people you've hurt from your rash, unthinking act. You've not only hurt Flower and me, but how about all my patients? Like Mrs. Primcastle and Mr. Whimpleman. There's hardly a family in Foster Flat that hasn't come to me at some point in time in the last several years."

"You're right. It was rash and thoughtless of me, but I'm sure there must be something I can do to rectify matters."

"Like what?"

"I don't know," Harper admitted. "Not yet, but give me time. I'll come up with a solution."

"Well, in the meantime, I think it would be a good idea for you to find somewhere else to eat your meals," Fatima said, standing up and brushing off her jeans. "Come on, Flower. We have a long trek to make...alone!"

"But I can't walk all the way down the mountain," her daughter objected.

"I know, but it's downhill, and I'll carry you most of the way. We'll do fine by ourselves. We've managed so far in our life. We'll manage now."

"That won't be neces..." Harper started, but then stopped as Fatima glared angrily at him. "Okay, have it your way." He watched as Fatima and Flower started down the mountain, finally calling out. "When did the letter say he'd be coming?"

"A week from Monday," Fatima called back over her shoulder without stopping.

HARPER AWOKE AT EXACTLY 3:33 on Wednesday morning. He lay in bed staring at the digital clock next to his bed until it flipped over to 3:34. He'd been awakened by a crazy idea that wouldn't let him go back to sleep. He finally arose and fixed himself a cup of coffee. The more he thought about the idea, the crazier it seemed and yet, the more enrolled he became. After all, it was already Wednesday, and they were running out of time for a solution. *It might just work,* he thought, as he sipped the steaming brew. He pulled out a pad of paper and started making notes on how to turn the crazy idea into a workable solution that would get the Board of Medical Examiners off Fatima's back.

At 7:05 AM, he leaned back in his chair. "It might just work," he muttered to himself. "Hell, it's got to work." He jumped up, threw on some clothes and headed to the Apothecary, where he found Fatima checking out some of her morning patrons. He waited in line until it was his turn.

Fatima looked up from the cashier with a broad smile that quickly disappeared when she saw him. "What are you doing here? I thought I told you to find another place to take your meals."

He raised his hands in a sign of peace. "I'm not here to eat. I woke up this morning at exactly 3:33 with an idea on how to get the Board off your back. By the way, three is my lucky number, so it's got to be a good idea."

"You mean, you have figured out a way to get the Medical Board that you reported me to off my back? Why, isn't that so very kind of you."

"Listen, just give me ten minutes to explain my idea. If you don't like it, we don't have to do it, but I'm sure it'll work...well, kinda sure."

Fatima continued to stare at him for several seconds before grudgingly replying, "Okay, ten minutes, but that's it. Go back to my office. Cyndy will be here to relieve me in a few minutes."

Harper retreated to the small office customarily reserved for Fatima and her patients. As he waited, he went over what he wanted to say to persuade Fatima to go along with the idea. The more he thought about it, the more he began to question his own sanity, but then he reminded himself that time was running out. They had to try something, and this was the best idea—really the only idea—he'd been able to come up with thus far.

A few minutes later, Fatima walked in, with a scowl on her face. "Okay, Dr. Harper, you've got ten minutes before I call Mr. Whimpleman back here to toss you out."

Harper took a deep breath and refrained from wiping the perspiration he felt trickling down his face. "It's really simple," he began. "I'll take over your practice, so when Dr. Bastian arrives, all he'll see is a fully licensed medical doctor starting out in his new practice. He'll realize there's nothing to see here and he'll go home. Easy, peasy."

Fatima stood there in front of him for several seconds before bursting out laughing. "That's it? That's your solution? We'll lie to a state agency that has the power to arrest us and put us in jail for such an infraction. Brilliant! Just down-right brilliant...as in not, as in dumb, as in dumb and dangerous to boot." She glanced at her watch. "Well, you still have eight minutes. Is there anything else you want to say?"

"Listen to me. I know the idea may sound a bit radical when you first hear it, but it can work. It's got to work."

"And why is that?" Fatima asked, a note of curiosity in her voice.

"Because I've been a real jerk, calling the Board before I'd even met you or given you a chance, but now I have. I've got to make this right."

"So, this is really all about you, is it?"

"What? No! I mean, well sure, I want to make things right between us, but that's not all of it. In the last few days, I've had the opportunity to talk with sev-eral of your patients, and I've yet to find anyone who's had a bad thing to say about you. In fact, if I didn't know better, I'd swear you must be an angel or something. This town needs you."

"What about your practice?"

Harper hesitated before replying. "I don't know. Maybe I can still make a go of it. Honestly, I haven't thought that far ahead." He stood up and took a cou-ple steps towards her. He reached out and grasped her hand. "We can do this. I just know we can. Besides, this whole town will get behind you. This Bastion fellow won't have a clue what's going on."

"Well," Fatima said, as she slowly withdrew her hand from his, "it might work."

He opened his mouth to agree, but she stopped him. "But if it doesn't, you'll certainly lose your license to practice. Have you thought of that?"

Harper nodded. "Yes I have, but I'm willing to take that chance."

Fatima studied him for several seconds. "You'd do that for me? Why?"

He took her hand again. "Because in the few days I've known you and your daughter, I've realized you're good people, and I...well, I care about you both."

Fatima smiled for the first time as she reached up with her other hand and placed it on his. "You've suddenly grown all touchy feely, haven't you?"

"Oh, I'm sorry. I didn't mean..." He started to let go of her hand.

"No, no, that's okay. It's kinda nice," Fatima admitted. She glanced down at her watch. "You're time is almost up. Anything else?"

"Yes, just one other thing. Do you think there's any way you could spare a couple eggs over easy and some toast and bacon? I'm famished."

"STRANGER SIGHTED!" Flower yelled from atop the carousel horse at the front of the Apothecary, where Fatima had placed her as lookout.

"What's he look like?" Fatima asked as she stepped out from behind the counter.

"Large, fat man in a dark blue suit, who looks none too happy to be here," Flower replied.

"Okay, places everyone. Remember, it's just a typical Monday afternoon so act natural." Fatima removed the apron she'd been wearing to protect her flowered dress. It was time for her to change roles.

As the stranger entered, Fatima stepped forward with a gracious smile. "Good day. Welcome to the Apothecary. Would you like a table or would you prefer sitting at the counter?"

"Neither," the man replied gruffly. "I'm not here to eat. I'm Dr. Alexander Bastion from the State Board of Medical Examiners. There's been a complaint filed of illegal activity taking place at this address. I'm here to investigate."

"Oh, really," Fatima said with a startled look on her face that she'd been practicing for days. "There must be some mistake. Perhaps you're referring to Dr. Harold Harper's medical practice. As his part-time receptionist and assistant, I can assure you everything is completely above board and legal. We are all so pleased to have him decide to locate his practice in our fair town." She turned to the other patrons, many of whom were turned in their chairs, listening for their cue.

"Oh, yes, most certainly."

"He's a real gem."

"What a wonderful doctor he is."

Dr. Bastion looked first at Fatima and then at the patrons with a suspicious stare. "Really? Well, is Dr...?" He stopped suddenly and sneezed three times, each one more violent than the one before. He took out a handkerchief and blew his red nose. "Damn these allergies. How in the world can anyone stand to live in these god-forsaken mountains?"

Fatima opened her mouth to comment on his condition, but then remembered she was not the practitioner today.

"As I was saying, is Dr. Harper around?"

"Yes sir," Fatima replied. "He's in the back seeing patients. Would you like me to show you the way? He shouldn't be too long."

"Please," Dr. Bastion said. He wiped his runny eyes with a corner of the handkerchief before returning it to his pocket. "The sooner I can get to the bottom of this, the sooner I can get away from all this nasty pollen."

Fatima waved him forward in front of her. As the two of them walked to the back, she signaled to Cyndy standing at the rear of the restaurant, who quickly disappeared into the back to give everyone there a heads up. As Dr. Bastion entered the short hallway, Fatima said, "His waiting room is the second door to the right. No need to knock."

Dr. Bastion nodded. As he entered the room, Mr. Whimpleman looked up from the magazine he'd been pretending to read. Seconds later, a second door on the other side of the room opened, and out stepped Mrs. Primcastle. "Oh, Dr. Harper, you're just the best." She turned to Mr. Whimpleman. "Isn't he just the best? I'm already feeling better. Oh, hello, who are you?" she said, directing the question to Dr. Bastion.

"This is Dr. Bastion," Fatima replied. "He's here to see our Dr. Harper. Seems there's been a clerical error back in Raleigh. He's here to sort it out."

Dr. Bastion sniffled, taking out this handkerchief again. "Clerical error? Well, maybe. It wouldn't be the first time."

"Mr. Whimpleman, would you mind if Dr. Bastion sees Dr. Harper first?"

"No, no, not at all. It'll give me time to finish this article I'm reading. Go right ahead."

"Right this way then," Fatima said, as she escorted the doctor into the exam room. As they entered, she noticed Dr. Bastion looking at the diploma and medical license that had been taken from Dr. Harper's real office a couple days ago. He studied them for a moment before turning to Fatima. "Duke graduate, huh? Impressive, though I can't imagine why someone from Duke would come to such a podunk town as this."

Fatima felt her hackles rise from the comment, but suppressed her mounting anger. "Well, we're certainly glad he did."

She was about to make another comment when, once again, Bastion sneezed repeatedly. *Poor man, he really is suffering*, she thought. *No wonder he hates this area so much.* "Have a seat there, if you will," she said. "Dr. Harper will be right with you. In the meantime, if I may." She reached out with both hands and gently placed them on the doctor's temples and rubbed gently. "Just close your eyes," she instructed, with the soft voice she normally used only with her patients. "This will help relieve some of the pressure in your sinuses." She continued this for a minute or two, slowly moving to rub under his eyes and along the side of his nose. "How does it feel now?" she asked.

"Surprisingly better," Dr. Bastion replied, without opening his eyes.

"Just sit there for a minute." She walked over to the counter and pulled something out of one of the drawers. She returned to the doctor and placed a small bag around his neck. "These herbs will help your allergy."

Bastion opened his eyes, the look of suspicion once more on his face. "Really?" he asked. "How do you know that?"

Fatima felt her heart skip. *Damn! What did I just do?* "I've seen Dr. Harper prescribe them to several of his patients. They're harmless, I can assure you. Just give it a try."

Dr. Bastion was about to reply, when the door opened and in stepped Dr. Harper.

"And what do we have here, Fatima? A new patient?" Dr. Harper extended his hand. The two doctors shook hands.

"No, Doctor, this is a colleague of yours, Dr. Alexander Bastion. He's from the Board of Medical Examiners."

"Really? To what do I owe this honor, Dr. Bastion?" Fatima noticed his eyes flitted to the herbal bag around Bastion's neck and back to her. She shook her head and prayed he wouldn't draw any more attention to it.

"It seems my office may have made a clerical error. I was told we'd received a complaint that there was an illegal, unlicensed practitioner at this location."

"Well, as you can see," Harper pointed to the license on the wall, "I'm fully licensed to practice medicine in this state."

"Yes, I see. As I said, it may have been a clerical error. I'll check with my office." He glanced at his watch. "I've another complaint to check out in the

Boone area, but it's too late in the day to go that far. Where would you recommend I stay overnight?"

"There's a nice bed and breakfast on the edge of town called the Charm House," Fatima replied.

"That will suffice. I'll return in the morning before I head to Boone." He nodded to Harper before turning to Fatima. He reached up to take the bag from around his neck. "Thank you for this Miss, but I'm a man of science..."

"That's okay," Fatima replied, smiling. "I won't hold it against you." She placed her hand on his hand holding the bag. "Leave it on overnight."

Dr. Bastion smiled for the first time. "Well, if you insist. I'll see you in the morning."

After Dr. Bastion left, Fatima and Harper stared at each other. Fatima let out a long sigh. Harper smiled. "So far, so good," he said.

"We're not out of the woods yet," Fatima countered.

"What was that thing hanging around his neck?"

"Don't ask," Fatima replied. "I'll see you in the morning for Act Two."

THE NEXT MORNING, THE cast members of the Foster Flat Players were once more in position. Everyone had been rotated to new seats and roles, just in case Dr. Bastion's powers of observation were more acute than they appeared, except for Flower, who once again served as the lookout.

"Here he comes again," Flower shouted. "Hey, look at that. He's smiling."

"Well, that's a good sign," Mrs. Primcastle said from her place at one of the front tables.

"Maybe," Fatima replied. "Or maybe he discovered our ruse and takes pleasure in closing down illegal operations. Whatever it is, we'll find out in just a minute. Break a leg everyone."

"Good morning, Ms. Flat. It appears your establishment is the most popular place in town," Dr. Bastion said, as he gazed around at the nearly full restaurant.

"Yes, we're quite fortunate in that regard," Fatima replied. "How are you feeling this morning, Dr. Bastion?"

"Fit as a fiddle," Dr. Bastion replied, "to borrow a quaint phrase from you mountain folk. I must confess, I wasn't looking forward to spending the night here. I figured my allergies would keep me awake all night long, but I slept like a baby."

"That's good to hear," Fatima said. "Would you care for some breakfast this morning, on the house?"

"Thank you, but that won't be necessary. Breakfast was included with my accommodations. That Mr. Haverstock was a gracious host, I must say. I understand now why he named his establishment the Charm House. No breakfast for me, but I do need to speak to Dr. Harper. I talked with my office this morning, and there appears to be some discrepancy that needs to be addressed."

"Oh, and what's that?" Fatima asked, trying to sound calm, while her insides began to churn.

"I'd like to discuss it with Dr. Harper, if you don't mind," Dr. Bastion said. "You're welcome to stay and join in the conversation."

Fatima nodded. *What did he find out from his home office? Had he uncovered other complaints that had been filed against her that she wasn't aware of?* "Right this way. I don't believe he's started seeing patients yet."

The two of them wove their way through the rows of tables and back to the waiting room, where they found Dr. Harper organizing the magazines.

"Good morning, Fatima. Oh, good morning, Dr. Bastion. You're up bright and early this morning."

"Yes, I need to get to Boone, but before I go, there appears to be an error in your file."

"My file?" Dr. Harper asked noncommittally.

"Yes, according to our records, your medical practice is actually located at the corner of Fifth Street and Justice, but this address is Main and Third. That would put your practice several blocks from here." Dr. Bastion was no longer smiling.

Dr. Harper shot a quick glance to Fatima and then back to Bastion. *Think of something to say,* Fatima thought, but nothing came to mind. She waited and prayed.

After a long pause that felt like it would drag on into the next day, the silence was finally broken by Harper's laughter.

"What's so funny?" Dr. Bastion asked sternly.

"Oh, nothing, I guess," Harper replied. "Clearly you've caught me."

Oh, God, no. He's not going to confess, is he? We were so close, Fatima thought. *Say something—anything!*

"It's my fault," she blurted out.

"Really? Your fault? Dr. Bastion turned to her, but before she could reply, Harper interrupted.

"No, really, it's on me. You see," he threw a warning look at Fatima, "I'm the one that failed to notify the Board of my change of address."

"Your change of address?" Fatima and Dr. Bastion said at the same time.

"Yes, you remember, Fatima. When I found out how much the rent was at Dr. Plimpton's old office, you were kind enough to offer this space, at least until I could get on my feet. I meant to call the Board to let them know, but in the rush of the move and all, well, I forgot."

"Really?" Dr. Bastion asked. He stared first at Dr. Harper, then to Fatima. Once again, time stood still. Then, he smiled. "Well, that explains everything. I'll simply notify the office of the change of address, and we can call the matter closed."

Fatima and Harper both let out a long breath. "I'm so sorry to make you come all this way due to my absent-mindedness," Harper said.

"Oh, that's okay. Like I said, I have another matter in Boone, so I had to make the trip anyway. Besides, if I hadn't come here, I might never have discovered a treatment for my allergies."

Harper looked at the other doctor with a confused look on his face.

"I took the liberty of offering him one of your home remedies," Fatima explained. "I'm so glad it worked."

"It did indeed," Dr. Bastion said. "It did indeed. Well, I need to get on the road." He turned to leave, but then stopped. "You know, you two should think about going into business together. You'd make quite a team."

"What?" Harper and Fatima said together.

"Look, I wasn't born yesterday," Dr. Bastion continued. "I suspect this little sack isn't Dr. Harper's treatment, but your own. It's my view that there's a place for alternative or complementary forms of treatment as long as the practitioner stays within the laws of the state in which they practice. Like I said, your two approaches complement each other. The folks of Foster Flat could really benefit from such a collaboration. Just something to think about. Now, I'll get out of your hair." With that, he turned and walked out, leaving Fatima and Harper staring at each other in amazement.

After he'd left, the two of them collapsed into chairs with a mixture of relief and exhaustion running over them. "We did it," Harper finally said.

"We sure did," Fatima replied. "I thought for sure you were going to confess."

"Yes, and I thought you might, as well."

The two of them sat in silence for a couple more minutes. Finally, Harper spoke up.

"Well, what do you think?"

"About what?"

"About his idea that we team up together."

Fatima stared at him. "Are you serious?"

"Sure, why not?" Harper replied. "After all, it's the townsfolk that would benefit the most. It's like Bastion said, our different approaches to healing don't have to compete against each other. They can be complementary."

Fatima slowly nodded. "That's true. My great-grandfather used to say, 'You can't fix everything broken around a home with the same tool.'"

"Exactly," Harper said. He leaned forward and took one of her hands in his. "That brings me to another subject I've been meaning to talk to you about."

"What's that?"

"Flower's ankle," Harper said.

"What about it?"

"Well, have you ever had an experienced orthopedist examine her?"

"No, not really," Fatima replied. "Dr. Plimpton checked her once or twice, but it was beyond him. He suggested I take her to Duke, but he didn't offer much hope for it. Why do you ask?"

"It just so happens my father is one of the best orthopedic surgeons in the world. He can be a real pain in the ass sometimes, but I feel certain he could help her. I'd be happy to set up an appointment for her."

As Fatima sat staring at him, she felt a seed of hope start to germinate in her heart. "I don't know what to say," she started. "That's awful kind of you, but honestly, I don't know how I'd ever be able to pay for your father's services.

"Well, let me worry about that. I'm sure I can persuade him to give you the ol' Harper family discount, and we'll work it out from there. I noticed earlier today that you have a couple rooms out back that don't appear to be used for anything but storage. Maybe we take Dr. Bastion's advice and move my offices here for real."

Fatima thought about his offer for another moment. "That could work. I've been meaning to clean that junk out anyway. As for having your father see Flower, I'd want to talk to her about it first."

"Fine," Harper said, as he stood up. "Let's go talk to her." He offered her his hand.

"What? Now?"

"Sure, why not? Besides, we need to let everyone, including Flower, know that this was the last performance of the Foster Flat Players for the foreseeable future."

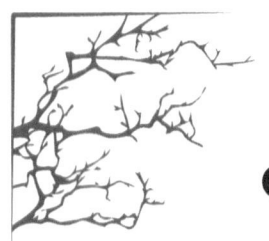

GIFT RETURNED

The chilling wind blew the scrap of paper against the frozen curb and just out of Jesse's grasp for the third time. His slick-bottomed tennis shoes slid across the icy surface of the street, threatening to set him hard on his behind. At the last second, he caught his balance and, in another moment, grabbed the blue crumpled paper in his painfully cold hands.

His hands were so cold that they ached and were stiff. Slowly, he managed to straighten the paper out and stared down at the scrawl. He hadn't dared to hope that the paper would be what it appeared, but as he read across the lines, his heart skipped several beats. It was a check, a signed check, made out in the amount of four hundred dollars. More money than he, in his short life, could ever remember seeing even cumulatively. The check was made out to Emily Lawson. *Not a blank check,* Jesse thought, *but still, there must be some way to cash it.* He flipped the check over and was amazed to find that the check had been signed neatly on the back by none other than Emily Lawson.

Hell fire, it'd be a snap to cash, wouldn't it? Jesse tried to remember what his mom had told him about checks, but for the life of him, he couldn't remember for sure whether the check was good. It was signed, both on the front and back. It was dated December 25, 1990. All the lines were filled out except the one on the lower left, but that didn't have to be filled out, did it? Jesse didn't think so. Well, his mom would know if the check was any good, and if it was, she'd pass easy enough for Emily Lawson. That could just as easy be a black name as a white one.

And boy, will this make Mom happy. It was gonna be a bodacious Christmas after all. Not only would they have a place to stay this year, but there'd be presents for all three kids and plenty to eat as well. *How far would four hundred dollars go?* Jesse wondered. *Ought to go pretty far.* Hadn't his mom just bought a whole house from the City for twelve hundred? Of course, the house was a might worse for wear, but it was the first home he and the rest of his family had ever owned. With four hundred dollars, they could do plenty to make it livable, couldn't they?

As Jesse thought about the old shack his mom had gone and spent their life fortune on, the four hundred dollar check shrank in size. Hell, his mom would end up spending the whole amount without blinking an eye and with no presents for any of them. *Maybe I can get it cashed myself without telling anyone. Then I'll go and spend it like it ought to be spent, not on no dumb shack.*

But the check was written out to a woman and ain't no way anyone would give no little black boy that much money. No way. He'd have to tell his mom and she'd do with it as she would. Still, they'd be better off than they were fifteen minutes ago before Jesse started chasing the blue scrap of paper down the street.

Meanwhile, if I don't hurry up, I'll be late getting home from school, and Mom will skin me alive, check or no check, Jesse thought, as he raced down the street towards the bus stop, hoping he hadn't missed the four o'clock bus. If so, he'd have a long wait ahead and a lot of explaining to do when he got home. As he rounded the corner, he saw the bus just pulling in to the bus stop and three or four people waiting to climb on board. This was certainly his lucky day. No one else was ever at this particular bus stop waiting on that particular bus. Never before. Then again, he'd never found four hundred dollars just lying on the street waiting to be picked up and spent. *Yes sir, today is my lucky day.*

"You heard what I said. We're going to return it to Ms. Lawson. It ain't our money. It's hers."

"But, Mom," Jesse wailed. "Finders keepers . . ."

"Now don't start your shenanigans. We may be poor folks, there can be no doubt, but we're honest too. You did a good deed today chasing down this slip of paper, but it's only a good deed if you finish the job. It goes back to Ms. Emily Lawson."

Jesse glared, first at his mom, then at Jessica and Jamie, his younger sister and brother, who were snickering under their breath.

"Well, there's no telling where she is, and there ain't no way to track her down," Jamie declared, with a smug look on his face.

"Simple enough," his mom retorted. "There's a name and phone number of the person who wrote the check. I'll just call her and tell her that my honest and caring son found Ms. Lawson's check and wants to return it to her. It's that easy."

"Yeah. It's always easy to lose money. When we going to start finding a way to keep some of it?"

"Hush child, I don't want to hear any more out of you. We've not done so badly. You three children are in school getting an education that I never had, and we finally have a roof over our heads that isn't paid for by the state."

"This old shack is so run down, the roof is likely to come down on our heads and knock all the foolish book learning right out of your three children," Jesse retorted, then ducked just in time to avoid the damp dish rag his mom had been using to wash the few plates they'd acquired in the last few weeks.

Jesse shuddered despite the heat coming from the dying embers of the charcoal that had served to cook their hotdogs, as well as to provide what little heat there was in the house. He glanced at the bag his mom had brought home with her this evening. How long did she expect them to live in this drafty old place, trying to stay warm on a half dozen lumps of charcoal at a time?

Sometime he wondered if she had good sense, but despite himself, he had to admire her determination to raise her children without outside support. *Maybe she is crazy and stubborn*, he thought, but she was also the only person he knew from the street that had managed to save twelve hundred dollars to buy their own house. He stared around the dark corners of the room, only partly lit by the dying embers and three stubby candles. And they were about to give back four hundred dollars to some woman who'd probably turn out to be white and have so much money she wouldn't even notice it was missing.

The four of them sat on the cold concrete steps of the red brick house that the voice over the phone had given as the home of Ms. Emily Lawson. Jesse gazed across the street at the line of neatly trimmed lawns and the multicolored Christmas lights. The Lawson house was the only one on the block without its lights on, although there were a gracious plenty lining every one of its straight edges.

Probably spends four hundred a month on her electric bill, Jesse thought, as he slipped his hands under his rump to give his cold cheeks a break from the hard and chilly surface. "Why do we have to spend the whole night out here freezing ourselves to the bone waiting for some silly woman who can't hold onto her own money?"

"Hush your mouth, Jesse, 'fore I have to give you something worth complaining about. Ms. Lawson is probably just working late, with it being the Christmas season and all. The lady on the phone said she usually gets home about this time."

"Couldn't you have just told the other lady where Ms. Lawson could come if she wanted the check? Why do we have to be the ones sitting out in the cold?"

"Lord, child, no one would have ever guessed you've spent most of your life out on the street, the way you carry on 'bout a little weather. We're waiting for Ms. Lawson here because I want to be sure we get the money to her as soon as possible. No need for us to be tempted by it. Besides, it's a good bit safer for us to travel to her than it would be for her to come into our neck of the woods. Look, there's the bus pulling up down the street. I bet that'll be her getting off now."

But the few people that got off the bus headed in the opposite direction. "Oh, well, it won't be long. Just be a little patient," Jesse's mom said in a quiet voice, as she pulled the worn collar of her jacket tighter around her neck.

And she was right. In less than ten minutes, a blue sedan pulled around the corner where the bus had been and stopped in front of the brick house. A short, stout lady with strawberry red hair climbed out from behind the wheel and waddled up the sidewalk. Jesse groaned. Just as he'd thought. They were getting ready to give the money he'd found to a whitey.

"Why, you all must be the Capel family. Loreen called me at work and told me you had called her. My word, I never expected to see that check again. It was so foolish of me . . ."

She continued to ramble on as she unlocked the front door with a large ring of keys.

"Come in, Ms. Capel. All of you, come in and get yourselves warm. I'll fix us some hot chocolate."

Hot chocolate! Jesse thought, and his mouth drooled. How long had it been since his last hot chocolate?

"Don't you bother none, Ms. Lawson. We can't stay. I just wanted to get your money back to you in case you needed. . ."

"It won't be no bother. I'd like some myself. It's the least I can do. Which one of your children found the check?"

Ms. Capel pushed Jesse forward, pulling his shoulders back as she did so to get him to stand up straighter.

"My oldest one here. Jesse, tell Ms. Lawson how you found it."

Jesse stared down at the worn toes of his tennis shoes and mumbled something unintelligible.

"Stand up straight and don't talk to your shoes," Ms. Capel said in her I-mean-business voice.

Jesse forced himself to take his eyes off the floor and spoke louder.

"It was in the street, like someone had thrown it away. I figured my little brother and sister could finally have a real Christmas if I could only catch it before my hands froze."

"Enough of that silliness," his mom scolded him.

"Well, you were a very brave little boy," Emily Lawson said. "I think you deserve the largest mug of hot chocolate."

Four hundred dollars for a mug of chocolate. What a trade.

Emily turned to his mother. "What can I do to repay you for your kindness?" she asked as she handed the second mug to her.

"Nothing. Really, nothing at all. It's just the Christian thing to do," she replied, as she took the steaming mug and sipped carefully on the hot brew.

"Nonsense. You and your son deserve to be rewarded. There aren't many people in the world who would do what you're doing. Not many at all."

You can say that again, thought Jesse. *Leave it to my mom to do the right thing even if her children go without presents this year. No wonder we've spent so many years on the street.*

"Well, there is one small thing you can do for us," his mom said, as she set her mug down on the table.

All right. Go for it, Mom. Ask her to buy us each a toy for Christmas. Don't forget I want a Walkman this year.

"If you wouldn't mind writing me a thank you note and sending it to our house. I'd like to have something the children can look at to remind them to always be honest."

Cripes sake! You've got to be kidding. A thank you note?

"I'll be happy to do that, but are you sure there's nothing else I can do?" Ms. Lawson asked, as she fetched a pen and paper to take down the address where to send the note.

"Nope. That's it. It'll be the first mail we've gotten. It'll be perfect."

EMILY LAWSON STARED at the dilapidated house, still finding it difficult to believe that the family she had met only a couple of days ago actually lived there. The house looked like it had been abandoned for years. Although there were still a few specks of paint here and there, for the most part, the house had obviously been ignored for a long time. The next door neighbor had said as much, once Emily finally convinced her that she was not a policewoman or from social services.

The elderly black lady had said someone had started living in the house a few weeks ago. The City had come out and removed the condemnation notice off the door and, in a few days, the Capel family had shown up. Emily remembered reading about the experimental housing project in the paper. The City was selling dozens of previously abandoned and condemned houses to anyone who would agree to bring them up to standard within a two year period.

But how in the world did Ms. Capel think she and her children could possibly do that? Emily wondered. *It'll take thousands of dollars and no telling how many hours of work. Hard work, and much of it skilled labor.*

Emily placed the thank-you note in the crack of the front door. As she did so, she stared through the dusty window once more. Someone was living there, all right. She could see a small hibachi grill sitting in the middle of the main room, where a small circular area had been swept away. The rest of the room and as much of the house as she could see through the cloudy window looked more like the remains left over from a hurricane or tornado.

She shook her head as she walked down the frozen path to the street. Already, an idea was blooming behind her teary eyes. The Capels were a hard working honest family. A family that deserved a change of luck. *Well*, Emily thought, *we'll just have to see what we can do about it.* By the time she arrived home, she'd already come up with a list of friends who owed her a favor. It was time to start collecting.

"WHAT ARE ALL THOSE trucks doing out front of our house?" Jesse asked, as they neared home.

"Hush, child. You think I'm some kinda psychic or something?" his mom said, as she slowed her stride, a worried look forming on her face.

Jesse shrugged his shoulders. He didn't know if his mom was a sigh-kick or not, since he had no idea what one was.

As the family started up the path to their home, the white lady with all the money and the delicious hot chocolate opened the door to their house and walked down the steps to meet them.

"Iffen you don't mind me asking, what are you doing in our house?" Jesse's mom asked, an edge of irritation just barely disguised in her voice.

"I sure hope you aren't angry with me," Ms. Lawson said. "I tried reaching you all day and, well. . . when I couldn't get you, I had to make a decision. These men are friends of mine." She pointed to the line of trucks. "They're here to help with your home. Mr. Deacon owns his own plumbing company and he's one of the ushers at my church. Jim Weatherspoon has the blue truck there. He's an electrician; one of the best in town, and Willie Struther does all sorts of odd jobs, including wallpapering and painting.

"I told them a little about you and your son's kind gesture. Each of them decided it would be a merrier Christmas for them if they pitched in and helped with a few things around the house. Besides, they all owe me a favor or two. This gives them a chance to start the new year with a clean slate."

Jesse's mom didn't say anything at first, just stood there facing Ms. Lawson, a look of confusion replacing the irritation. "I don't understand. Why are you doing this?"

Ms. Lawson slipped a plump arm around her shoulder and steered her toward the door, with the three kids following close behind. "Let's just say I'm returning the gift you gave to me."

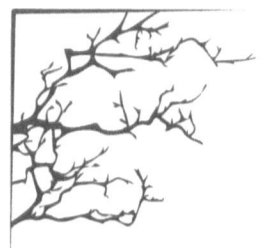

FRAGRANCE

C hristmas. Albert P. Flinnery's favorite time of the year, but not for the same reasons most people loved the holiday season. Albert didn't care about gift giving. Not that he was a scrooge or anything. He just didn't have many friends, except his fellow workers at the Foster Flat Sentinel, and most of them were stuck in the groove of passing around hard, tasteless fruitcakes. Ugh. He still had three of them taking up space in his freezer and a fourth one serving as an effective doorstop.

No, Albert P. Flinnery loved Christmas because, as a professional people watcher, the Yuletide season provided him with no end of interesting people to watch. People doing what people do best: acting strange, dressing in outlandish outfits, mixing and mingling—an exotic brew of quirky personalities.

Albert pushed himself away from the black enameled column that helped support the fourth floor of Stacey's Emporium, Albert's number one prime spot for people watching and story gathering. In a good year, Albert easily collected enough stories in the four weeks between Thanksgiving and Christmas to fill his weekly newspaper column through to the first week in August, when he made his annual fishing trip to Michigan. Between August and late November, he'd slide in fish yarns from his two-week vacation along with recirculated stories from the last twenty years at the Sentinel. Then, the cycle would begin again. Yes, the Christmas season made life pretty easy for Albert P. Flinnery, if not all that exciting.

Albert tossed the cigarette he'd been smoking down on the linoleum floor of Foster Flat's largest (and only) department store and studied the crowd. People watching was an art form for Albert. Not only did he make his livelihood from it, he lived for these precious few weeks. The trick was to mingle with the crowd without actually becoming part of the crowd. To notice everything while remaining unnoticed, a feat that Albert had taken to a masterful level.

He paused for a final moment with his knees slightly bent, watching for a small crack, a tiny imperfection in the river of people passing through the aisle. When it appeared, Albert expertly filled the gap, floating gracefully along the river of humanity. Periodically, he would adroitly step to the side, jot down a few notes, then step back into the river, to be carried gently downstream by the human current. As he was swept along by the river of warm, happy shoppers, it being still early in the day and the season, he felt in the pockets of his overcoat for the reassuring bulk of six small notebooks. He would have several of them filled before he left Stacey's in the late afternoon.

The fourth floor was one of his favorites. It contained a conglomeration of some of the most unusual gifts the fine purchasing agents of Stacey's could uncover. It attracted a large crowd of affluent shoppers, many from outside the area, and often some of the more exotic stories. Only one area of the department store could boast of better material—the bargain basement. But Albert didn't like to jump into his work too fast. He had developed a system, a flow. First, he'd stand off to the side and feel the crowd—get a sense of what was in the air for the season. It was always different, being influenced by many things: the economy, the political climate of the world, the new toys and gifts that had been Introduced since the previous season.

After tasting the season's atmosphere—a time of arousal for Albert, a little foreplay, so to speak—Albert would begin to mingle with the crowd, staying on the first three floors for most of the morning. He saved the fourth floor for just before lunch. It worked out nicely since his favorite eating place was also on the fourth floor. He found that the best time to eat was right at twelve, when the restaurant was splitting at the seams with people. Albert never worried. His special table was always waiting. It was one of the few extravagances he allowed himself. The table cost him two hundred bucks a season, a "tip" to Julio, the head waiter. It was worth every cent.

On this particular day, Albert was interrupted from his normal pattern by an especially interesting display of perfumes which was a bit unusual for the fourth floor, but it was not the location that attracted Albert's attention. It was the model demonstrating the cologne. She was drop-dead gorgeous. Now, being a professional people watcher, Albert was not easily taken in by beauty. He saw thousands of women every season that were attractive, hundreds that were pretty and dozens that were beautiful. But he had never in his forty-three years of people watching (he had started very early in life) seen such a breathtaking example of the opposite sex. The amazing thing was that she wasn't even his type. Albert preferred the erotic, sensual type, the ones with the big lips, the sad eyes, the husky voice, plus well-endowed feminine attributes.

This woman had none of those. She was blonde, while Albert preferred dark hair as a general rule, certainly not the platinum hue that haloed her head. Her lips were small and very red, and when she spoke, her voice was soft, barely more than a whisper, as though the small mouth could produce no larger volume. Her small frame was too petite for Albert's normal taste. No more than five feet or maybe five-two, her loose-fitting silk blouse made it difficult to detect her curves, but it was safe to say that voluptuous she was not.

Yet, Albert could not take his eyes off her. When he first saw her, he stopped dead in his tracks and was instantly pushed and shoved by a dozen shoppers. Albert knew better than to stop in the river of people. The crowd could be merciless when it came to those who tried to buck the currents. Besides, it drew attention, something Albert never did, but this time he couldn't help himself. The woman had taken his breath away.

Slowly, he edged his way out of the traffic flow and found another black column he could back up against for protection and where he could still watch her unnoticed. He lifted a cigarette out of the pack with his lips and lit it without thinking. It was several minutes before he could focus on anything else but her face. Finally, as the flame of the cigarette threatened to scald his lips, he spit the cigarette out and crushed it underfoot. Shaking his head slightly, he pulled a new pad out of his pocket, and wet his pencil.

But the pencil remained motionless over the paper. He noticed, for the first time, the details around the woman. She stood in the center of a display of fluffy clouds. In her hand, she held a small ivory bottle of spray cologne. With a low, wispy voice, she would ask each passerby if they would like to sample the new cologne. While Albert watched, he didn't see anyone refuse her. How could they? It would be like turning your own mother in for murder. It would be like spitting on the American flag. Iit would be . . . it would be impossible to refuse her anything, Albert thought.

Albert continued his vigil, concentrating on the small figure, his pencil poised over the notepad. After thirty minutes, he still had not taken a note, but he had begun to notice the people around the display. Many of the men and women passed the display, too busy to pay any attention to the lone figure, only to return in a few moments, a curious expression on their faces. Others would begin to shake their head negatively at her simple question, but would stop in mid-shake, their glare of annoyance changing to a simple, contented smile as they nodded their consent. Even the most obnoxious shoppers would pause for a few moments after the small bottle would pass a few inches from their face, leaving behind the most subtle fragrance. Then they would pass on, the lines of stress and discomfort melting away as they walked.

Amazing, Albert thought. *What could possibly smell so nice that it could have such an effect on so many people?* After a few more minutes, he decided there was only one way to find out. He slid back into the crowd and pushed his way towards the young woman.

She smiled pleasantly at him as he drew near and Albert felt his heart slip on its back like an anxious puppy. "May I offer you a small gift of a most refreshing fragrance?" she asked him, in the most melodious voice he had ever heard.

He could not answer at once, frozen like an idiot carved in ice, glazed eyes and all, smiling back at her. "Sir, may I offer you . . ."

Albert shook himself back to the present. "No...thanks, but I'd like to ask you a few questions, if I may. Do you have a time you take a break or . . ."

"Oh no, I don't take breaks. My work is never done, but I'd be happy to take a few moments for a reporter. Publicity is always welcome by . . . by my boss."

"How did you know . . . ?"

"Let's just say you get pretty perceptive at this job," she replied, her voice a blend of sleigh bells and wind chimes. "What may I help you with?"

"Tell me about your company and this new fragrance."

"Oh, it's not a new fragrance, not really. We've just found a new way to market it, that's all. Salvation has been around since the first Christmas."

"Catchy slogan you have there. Where did it come from?"

Her small lips parted slightly in a smile that sent a warm caress to Albert's heart. "Why, surely you know. The source of salvation is no secret. As the sign says, 'from Christian Deus.' Or to put it more simply, from Our Lord, Jesus Christ."

Albert started to laugh, but stifled it with a cough when he noticed the young woman apparently wasn't joking. "They certainly have you well programmed, but do you really think this promotion is in good taste, considering the time of year and all?"

The young lady replied without hesitation. "Why, of course it's in good taste. What better time of the year to introduce a new way to Salvation than on Christ's birthday. Lord knows it's long overdue. If you don't believe me, just look around at all the sin and suffering in the world. So unnecessary. I'm sorry," she continued as she glanced at the throng of people passing by. "I'm afraid I must get back to work. Many souls will be lost if I don't concentrate on my task. Could I offer you a small gift...?"

"Uh, no, I don't think so. Could I have your name, you know, for the article? I like to be able to quote my sources."

"Oh, sure, it's Angela."

"Cute, Angela," Albert said. He pretended to jot it down in his notebook, although he knew he would take it with him to his grave, securely locked in his memory along with a full-colored picture of her face. "They certainly have picked you well for the part."

"Why, thank you. I've worked hard to deserve this opportunity to serve the Lord. Please reconsider my offer. I'm sure you will be quite pleased."

"Maybe after lunch, Angela. After I check out the bargain basement. Hate to waste such a wonderful fragrance on those ruffians that congregate down in the pit."

Angela smiled once more at him. "Very well, sir. You know where Salvation is. Just be sure not to wait too long."

ALBERT FOUND HIMSELF distracted during his lunch, barely tasting the corned beef on rye that he usually relished. His mind kept returning to the mysterious Angela and the kind, loving smile that seemed to have taken seed in his heart and was now spreading its roots throughout his body. *Where does Madison Avenue come up with these ideas?*, he wondered. *Who would have thought to name a new cologne Salvation? Most of them were just the opposite—Obsession, Mystique, Erotic Night.*

Albert decided to check out the basement area, as was his regular routine, but then he'd return to ask Angela a few more questions. He paid his tab and started towards the escalator. It seemed easier to make his way through the crowd than usual, despite the fact that there were more people than he could remember ever seeing.

Everyone seems more cooperative this year, he thought, but then, it is the first day. They don't start getting really nasty until the week before Christmas. He wound his way down the escalator, stopping for a few moments at each floor to get a sense of the atmosphere. It was on the first floor that he began to sense a change in spirit.

He stood outside the traffic area near the escalator and tried to identify the change. It took him a few moments before he could put his finger on it. The first thing he noticed was the increased volume of noise. There was the same amount of background Christmas music and the bong, bong one always heard in a department store, but here on the first floor, there was something more. Finally, it came to him. Anger. The crowd felt discontented and unhappy; much more so then they had been on the fourth floor. There was more shoving and pushing and even some angry words being exchanged among strangers.

Guess more people in a rush to get home down here, he thought, but couldn't recall ever detecting such a difference in the various floors before, and the difference became more pronounced as he rode the escalator down to the basement.

Albert loved the bargain basement for several reasons. First, it was where a some of his best stories originated and from where much of his annual income was derived. Also, he experienced a sense of belonging when he visited the lower level of Stacey's. The common folk shopped in the bottom basement. In fact, that was the third reason Albert enjoyed visiting the basement. He could always make his few gift purchases without taking time out from his people watching, while rubbing elbows with his kind of people.

But this year Albert sensed a definite, though inexplicable difference in the mood of the basement. It could only be described as ugly. Everywhere he turned, crowds of people pushed and shoved, maliciously gouging at each other, fighting for the most horrible-looking pieces of merchandise. Faces of men and women contorted into angry scowls as they threw themselves at each other over the last pea green sweater or hot pink scarf.

My God, what's going on here? Albert wondered, as he stepped off the escalator. But before he could get his bearings, a large woman, resembling a defensive lineman, with multiple plastic bags clutched in her massive arms, barreled into him, knocking his breath away.

"Get outta my way," she shouted, shooting him an obscene gesture with her free hand. "Try for that coat, and I'll flatten you."

An already flattened Albert replied, "What coat?"

Without answering him, the woman gave him another vicious poke in the ribs, forcing him back several feet, where he cracked his head against one of the black enameled columns. Through the haze of stars, he could just make out the woman's plump arm as she reached out and yanked a khaki-colored army jacket off the rack near where Albert had been standing. As she passed by, she threw him a look that suggested she was about to finish him off with a swift karate chop to the neck, but just as suddenly, her attention shifted to another treasure at the far end of the store.

Grabbing reassuringly to the round column, Albert waited for his head to clear and to regain his composure. He circled around the column as though patrolling his own castle's defenses. No one else seemed to be paying him any attention at the moment, which gave him time to get his bearings.

As he studied the spectacle before him, his gaze fell on a display that took his breath away again. It was a remarkable replica of Dante's Inferno, or at least what Albert imagined Dante had envisioned. The mock flames flickered wildly at the lone figure who stood in the middle of them. The man was the typical tall, dark and handsome type one expected in department store displays, except for one minor point. As Albert stared at the dark features of the man, he detected the most malicious, evil countenance he had ever felt emanating from the stranger's eyes. Albert's breath caught in his throat as he spied the small object the stranger held in his hand—a cologne bottle with the word "SIN" boldly etched in the glass.

"Angela's competition seems to be alive and well in Stacey's bargain basement," Albert muttered to himself. He felt the tiny hairs along the back of his neck prickle when, with the uttering of the words he had barely spoken, the tall stranger looked in his direction, peered deeply into Albert's eyes and nodded, as a sardonic grin sliced across his handsome features.

The stranger raised his other hand, and with one long finger motioned Albert to come to him. Much to Albert's surprise, he found himself gliding towards the flames.

"Would you care to try a small sample?" the husky voice asked, as he continued waving Albert towards him.

"Who the hell are you?" Albert asked.

The man burst out with a roar of laughter that made Albert's skin crawl, as though the long nails of the man's hand had just scraped across a chalkboard.

"Who in the hell is right!" he cackled between peals of laughter. "Why, I'm Devlin, of course. So nice for the Sentinel to send its most distinguished reporter down to check out the common folk. Now, won't you try a sample of what everyone is dying to have under their tree this year? Yours, free of charge with no obligation. I know you're going to love it."

The finger continued to draw Albert nearer to the flames. Only in the last instant did Albert suddenly realize what was happening, as Devlin pointed the spray bottle at his face. The well-manicured finger depressed the small pump, the fine cloud of mist escaping from the tiny orifice, traveling straight for Albert.

At the final instant, Albert held his breath and ducked away from the approaching fumes. "Nooooo!" he screamed, falling to his knees. As he did so, he felt the heat of the flames and realized they weren't a clever trick of some slick Madison Avenue ad agent. They were real—the hottest flames straight from the bowels of the earth. Albert clawed his way between the forest of legs, fighting at the same time to regain his footing, desperately trying to find his way to the escalator.

But the angry crowd seemed to have other plans for Albert, as dozens of feet stomped his fingers, and knee after knee banged his head and crushed his ribs. "Albert, please," he heard Devlin's voice call from behind him. "Don't be so silly. Just give it a try—one little whiff. After all, you are one of the common people, aren't you?"

Albert heard the maniacal laughter again and felt he would scream and never stop if he did not escape at once. He stopped trying to regain his footing, instead crawling on all fours in the direction where he hoped to find the escalator. The thick crowd continued to inflict damage on his tired body. Within minutes, his hands were bloody, his nails cracked and broken, his ribs bruised and his head pounding from the vicious assault. Still, he continued crawling towards the escalator, praying he was headed in the right direction. His strength was almost completely drained before he caught a glimpse of the corrugated steps moving upward like a line of toy soldiers.

He grasped once, twice, a third time at the black rubber banister, then clung to it with his last ounce of strength as it pulled him up the stairway. He thought he felt a pair of hands with strong fingers and sharp nails clutch at his legs. He kicked out in a motion more like the throes of a dying fish than a kick and was relieved to feel the hold upon his legs release. The crowd on the escalator was still thick and mean, but as he neared the top on the first floor, he managed to pull himself to his feet.

He pushed through the bodies in front of him, not stopping at the first floor, nor at the second or third. He continued on past the neon sign of the fourth floor, ignoring the mounting shadows along the periphery of his vision, which threatened to blind him. He did not stop until he fell onto the soft clouds at Angela's feet and stared up into her crystal blue eyes.

"May I offer you a small gift of a most refreshing fragrance?" he heard her ask, in the same melodious voice. He nodded weakly, tears flowing down his cheeks. As the fine mist descended upon him, Albert collapsed, his head resting on one of Angela's small feet. The mist of Salvation floated gently down upon his hot brow. She was right. It was most refreshing.

DIVINE DISORDER

The shockwave sweeps through the seed packet without warning, throwing the world into a topsy-turvy chaos and my carefully laid life plans into the compost bin. One minute, we're in the master gardener's son's pudgy hand. The next moment, one of his mobile roots trips over a crack in the cement walkway leading to the garden where Sela and I were to spend our life intertwining our roots together. As the packet slips from his hand, I'm suspended in free fall. Time slows. I see my beloved soulmate, Sela, floating above me along with dozens of other seeds, just before we crash into the sidewalk... hard.

Time accelerates as though trying to catch up with itself. I remember the deafening wail of the boy, but mostly I remember hearing my own shout, "This isn't going well," as a bunch of us are catapulted out of the packet, including my best friend, SK. "Not going well at all," I scream as I fly through the air, bouncing along the cement and into a crack in the sidewalk. I lie there dazed, a bit bruised, but mostly uninjured. Then, I notice the gardener has arrived on the scene. He picks up his son, brushes off the little boy's pants, and dries the tears running down his son's face. He starts to walk off, then stops to pick up the seed packet and continues to the garden...without me!

This can't be happening. I yell, scream, cry, and plead—all to no avail. This is not how my life is supposed to play out. I was at the top of the pack. It was my turn. I'd just missed out the season before. I'd even been in the gardener's palm about to be planted into the fertile ground, but, at the last moment, he had poured my comrades and me back into the pack, where we sat for an interminable time.

And now, here I am missing all the action again. I look around, but all I can see is dirt and debris that has accumulated in the crack. *Great*, I think. It's not bad enough to fall into a crack in the sidewalk. I've rolled into a thin crevice within the crack surrounded by some of the worst excuses for dirt I've ever seen.

"Not fair, not fair, not bloody fair," I scream. "Get me out of this damn crack!" I keep shouting until, finally, I hear a familiar voice from above.

"Is that you, Seedmore? Are you okay?"

"That you, SK? I'm down here in this hellhole of a crack. Where are you? Do you see Sela?"

"I'm just above you, Seedmore. I saw you fall. There are quite a few others up here, but no Sela."

Great, my soulmate and I have been thrown apart by fate. This has got to be the worst day of my life.

Days pass without any change, except in my mood, which grows darker as I face the brutal reality that I may die in this God-forsaken crevice. SK tries to cheer me up, but I'll have none of it. By the third day, I'm ready to feed him to a bird, anything to get him to stop his New Age aphorisms.

"All is not in Divine Order," I shout at him, venting my anger and frustration the only way I know. "If it were, I'd be lying snuggly under a half-inch of quality topsoil with Sela nearby, not in this hellhole of malnourished dust. I had my life with Sela all planned out, so kindly shut up about this being in Divine Order!"

SK mumbles a few inarticulate words, then, when I don't respond, he grows quiet. I drift off into my own world, dreaming about growing up in the garden next to Sela, eventually sharing our pollen and creating the next generation of seeds. When I finally emerge from my melancholy, I'm surprised how dark it has become. Surely it's not nighttime already. I gaze up to the small slit of sky I can see, and notice storm clouds building. Oh, great. Now what? But before my newest pity party gets into full swing, it's interrupted by a flash of lightning, followed a split second later with a loud clap of thunder. "Super, now I'm going to get rained on. What's next, God—mildew?" The Foster Flat area is known for its storms that suddenly appear in the late afternoon. It looks like I'm about to experience one.

Sure enough, within minutes I hear the first patter of raindrops and then the bottom falls out. It's what the gardener would call a gully washer, and unfortunately, it does just that, sweeping SK and the other seeds away. I hold my breath in anticipation of joining them. After all, anywhere has to be better than where I am, but once again my life is a product of "Divine Disorder." As the rain continues to fall, I feel a tremor around me as the sides of the crevice collapse, throwing me into darkness.

Crud.

Days pass. I lose count of the number of times the ground warms, then cools, and then warms again—certainly more than a week, more likely two or even three. I notice the ground has grown warmer. With the warmth, and moisture from the rain, and the darkness, I feel...different.

My coarse outer protective shell has softened, and I feel myself begin to swell. Then, one morning I awaken to feel my own vestigial appendages digging into the poor excuse for soil that has become my prison.

Oh, no, this can't be happening. I'm starting to grow. Not here! Anywhere but here. Well, not anywhere. I'm supposed to be growing next to Sela, maybe with SK as our next-door neighbor, but not here in this miserable excuse of a crack. Man, I just can't catch a break. Then, I remember an argument I'd had with SK just a day or two before he'd been washed away.

"I don't believe in accidents, Seedmore. I really don't."

"Well, these last few days must have blown that belief out of your head by now."

"No, not really. You see, in a no-accident Universe, we're all here for a purpose, and our job is to make the most of each and every situation we find ourselves in, including the unexpected ones, like the one we find ourselves in right now."

Could SK have been right? Could there be some greater purpose to all this? After all, despite everything, I am still alive. Not only alive but also growing. Yeah, growing, but look where I'm growing. How can I possibly fulfill my greater purpose here in this crack? SK was a cool dude, but he didn't know what he was talking about. Or did he?

I remember SK's platitude that made me the angriest: "All is in Divine Order, so surrender to what is." What if I did just that? What if I tried surrendering to this situation, at least for a couple of days, while at the same time trying to be the best seed I could be, growing in a crevice of a crack? I mean, what harm could come from it? After all, there's no one else around to notice if I fail, so what do I have to lose?

A couple of days turn into a couple of weeks, and before I know it, I find I'm squeezing myself above the crack into the brightness and warmth of spring.

I can't believe I'm saying this, but life hasn't been so bad these last few weeks. Oh, there's the occasional close call from being almost squashed by a passing pedestrian, but, well, hey, you know what they say. "That which doesn't kill you makes you stronger." Oh, God, another one of SK's aphorisms. Man, I miss that seed.

Uh-oh, here comes that kid again.

The gardener's kid jogs down the walkway on his way to the garden, when he suddenly stops and bends down to me. His face is gigantic and his voice thunderous. "Daddy, Daddy. Look at this one. It looks like some of the plants in the garden."

I feel the tremor of the ground as the gardener pauses in his weeding and walks over to admire his son's astute observation. "Some people call seeds that take root in unusual places like that 'volunteers'. Sometimes you'll find a seed growing from the previous year's plants, or simply find one growing in unexpected places. I think of them more like orphans."

"Like me, Dad?"

"Well, like you and me. Remember, I was raised in an 'unexpected place', as well."

The kid bends down close to me again. "But what if someone steps on it? We gotta help it, Dad."

What's he talking about, helping me? I've grown pretty comfortable where I am.

"Well, I don't know if we can dig down to get enough of the root system..."

Exactly my point. I feel a nervous twitch in my roots just thinking about it.

"I can, Dad. Just like you saved me, I'm going to save this plant."

"Well, I suppose it's worth a shot. Let's go get you some smaller digging utensils from the kitchen."

For the life of me, I can't think of any of SK's sayings that will help me in this situation, so I decide to pray for another thunderstorm, anything that will keep the two gardeners from digging me up. Of course, it remains a bright and sunny day. My luck is holding.

Holy Cow! Here they come. Boy, those utensils from the kitchen look mighty big and sharp. Hey kid, don't mess with the roots. Watch out there. Really, this isn't a good idea, my boy. I've gotten used to this spot.

But the kid keeps working on the soil around me, and I have to admit, he's much more careful than I'd expected him to be. Suddenly, I feel the ground below me loosen, and the next thing I know, I'm moving.

Wait a minute. Where are you taking me? Oh, shit. Here I go again. All is in Divine Order...all is in Divine Order...surrender, surrender.

Can it be? Is that what I think it is? It is. It's the garden. He's taking me to the garden. Oh, my God, SK was right. There really are no accidents, just a whole lot of mystery. But, wait a minute. Where are you planting me? Not here. Where's my Sela? That's not Sela. I'm supposed to be with Sela, remember?

I look around and see SK the next row over.

"Hey, SK. It's me, Seedmore. Have you seen Sela?"

"Well, I'll be. It is you. Welcome to paradise. I wasn't sure I'd ever seen you again."

"It'll be paradise as soon as I find Sela."

"Gosh, I don't know how to break it to you, but I don't think Sela made it. I've been here since the rain carried me out of the crack and deposited me here, but I haven't seen Sela at all. I'm so sorry, Seedmore. I know you and she were close."

"Yeah, we were soulmates. At least I thought we were." No Sela? How can I be expected to go on with my life without my soulmate? The thought of living without Sela is devastating to me, but I don't know what I can do about it. It's beginning to feel more like Divine Discontent taking over again. How am I supposed to give up on a dream that I've had...well, forever?

I look around at the other tomato seedlings. Most of them are a good bit taller than me, a product of the rich garden loam they've been planted in, except the one closest to me, who is more or less my same size. As I'm getting familiar with my surroundings, I hear a melody. At first, I think it's angels singing to me, then I realize the gardener has turned on his transistor radio.

As I listen to the words of the song, I realize God does, indeed, work in mysterious ways, for the lyrics speak directly to me: "If you can't be with the one you love, honey, love the one you're with." Sounds like another one of SK's platitudes. When you really love another, it's just not that easy to let go and start loving someone else. I'm not so sure I'm ready to give up my dreams of a life with Sela. Still, life goes on, so I may as well at least get to know the other plants that I am destined to spend the season with.

I turn to the small seedling next to me.

"Hello there. My name is Seedmore, what's yours?"

There's a long pause before my neighbor answers me.

"I didn't think you recognized me, Seedmore, but that's okay. I didn't recognize you at first either. I'm Sela."

"Oh, my God, how can that be? You were one of the most robust seeds of the pack. What happened?"

"Like you, I also suffered many hardships after being thrown from the pack. It was a difficult journey, but you know what they say..."

As we turn our leaves towards the sun, we answer at the same time, "What doesn't kill you, makes you stronger." I guess we've both been hanging out with SK too long. Foster Flat is a fantastic place to live if you don't mind the twists and turns of its mountain magic.

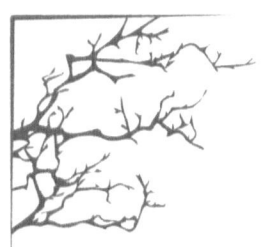

BEARFOOTING

May is a month of unpredictable weather in the North Carolina mountains, as are the other eleven months of the year, so it's not all that surprising that mama bear and her cub were caught by the late afternoon thunderstorm on the wrong side of the river from their customary shelter. Mama bear, with her cub riding on her back, was only a third of the way across the river when the bottom fell out. Within moments, the water around them transformed from a placid flow to a raging river of angry, dirty water that swept the cub from her back. Alarmed, mama bear swam after her cub, fighting to stay afloat until a tree limb struck her from behind, almost knocking her unconscious. She found herself fighting for her own life as she caught glimpses of her cub floating downstream, clinging to another piece of debris, his plaintive cries ripping at her heart.

LACY TURNER AND HER husband, Nick, were enjoying the last day of their mountain getaway before returning to the normal routine of their lives back in civilization. As Lacy crawled out of their two-person tent, she stood up and stretched, feeling her stiff back muscles complain pleasantly with the movement. She watched the sun slowly ascend above the mountain peaks as she breathed in the crisp morning air. It had been quite a night, with so much wind and rain she'd been fearful they'd be blown away inside their tent. Luckily, Nick had done a more than adequate job staking down the tent, as well as locating it far enough from the stream, which had grown into a raging river in a matter of minutes.

She turned her attention towards the river. It had crested during the night and was slowly returning to its natural state. That's when she noticed the small black package that had been delivered on her doorstep. At first, she thought it might be another camper's furry jacket, until it moved.

"Oh, my God," Lacy said as she realized the object was alive. She tapped on the top of the tent. "Nick, wake up. We have a visitor," she said, before running down to get a better look at the new arrival.

"Honey, I know how much of an animal lover you are. It's one of the things I find most endearing about you," Nick said, trying once again to talk some sense into his wife. "But we're not equipped to nurse a bear cub back to health."

"But we can't just leave the poor thing out here alone," Lacy pleaded.

"You're not listening to me," Nick replied, then, realizing how argumentative that sounded, added, "Dear, there's a very well run nature science center back in Asheville that will be able to take much better care of him than we can. It's right on the way home, or at least not much out of our way."

Lacy glanced down at the bedraggled little bear that had hardly moved since she first found him. "Her," Lacy said.

"What?"

"I think it's a female," Lacy replied.

"Whatever." Nick could feel himself growing impatient, so he took a deep breath.

"What will happen to her after that?" she asked.

"They'll nurse him...I mean her back to health and then release her to the wild, or they'll give her a home at the center. In either case, she'll have a much better life there than she would with us."

Lacy slowly nodded. "I guess you're right," she finally conceded. "It's just that she's so cute."

Cute now, Nick thought, *but just wait a few months. By the end of the summer, she'll be bigger than our Mastiff back home. What a pair that would be.* Instead, he said, "I know, and that's why we want to be sure to get her to the nature center as soon as possible. If you'll start breaking down our campsite, I'll load her in the back of the pickup. Once we're in cellphone coverage again, I'll call and let them know we're bringing her in."

THERE'S A MYTH THAT circulates among the longtime residents of Foster Flat that there's an energy—some say magical, others prefer spiritual,but all agree it's a strange energy—that attracts just the right people, who are pulled like a magnet to the small mountain town. Could it have been that same energy that awoke our small bear cub just outside the Foster Flat town limits while the Turners stopped to get a bite to eat and to fill up with gas? In any case, she woke to a myriad of strange odors, including the delectable scents of food that had her stomach growling and her mouth salivating from hunger.

She stood up in the bed of the pickup truck and stuck her nose in the air to get a better sense of the direction the food aromas were coming from. Having made the determination, she scurried out of the back of the truck and started towards the rear of the diner. As she did so, she picked up a second scent that she'd smelled only once or twice before. Humans! Her mother had warned her of the danger. Come to think of it, where was her mother? She stuck her nose in the air again and took in a long inhalation. Nothing. Not the slightest whiff of her scent. Then she recalled the storm of the previous evening, clinging tightly to her back as they crossed the river, then suddenly being swept away from her. The rest became foggy and muddled until waking a few minutes ago. *I'll have to go look for her...right after I get a little something to eat*, she thought, as she continued to the rear of the diner where the food smells appeared strongest.

Her head and half her body were well inside the metal trash can when she heard the screeching of a door in desperate need of oiling, followed a second later by the screaming of one of the short order cooks.

"Get the hell out of my trash," Elbert Schroder shouted, as she grabbed the broom next to the door reserved for just such a purpose. "This is the third time this month I've had to clean up after you varmints, and I have had it with you."

Adrenalin pumped through the bear cub's body as she started to pull herself out of the trash, lost her balance and fell to the pavement with trash cascading all around her.

Time to leave, she thought as she saw the big man with a stick in his hand advancing on her. She ran in the other direction, still smacking her lips, enjoying the taste of the discarded cinnamon rolls. She continued running, feeling better for having at least partially filled her stomach, and enjoying the freedom of being alive, despite being on her own. She didn't slow to a walk until she was well inside the town limit of Foster Flat.

The bear cub meandered through the neighborhood outside Foster Flat proper, visiting two or three trash cans along the way. While she remembered her mother warning her to stay away from anywhere that the human scent was strong, the lesson didn't make much sense to her at the moment. After all, where else could you find such delectable food so readily available? No need to climb a tree for the berries, or spend all that time trying to corner a fish in the stream. All you had to do was flip off the lid of the containers that were abundantly available to discover what treats awaited inside. By the time she'd made it through the outskirts of the town, her stomach was full and it felt like the perfect time to take a nap. She found an outcropping of pine trees between two of the houses with a thick layer of needles that made a most comfortable bed. Despite the many human odors all around, she was asleep within minutes.

By the time she awoke several hours later, the sun had set and a nearly full moon had risen, with beams of light filtering through the trees above. At first, the cub was disoriented and thought she was back in the lair that had been her and her mother's home, but then remembered the cave's floor wasn't nearly as soft as the one beneath her now. But that wasn't the only hint that alerted her to her new environment. Her mother was absent, not only her physical presence but also her smell. The rush of memory cascaded over the cub. She was on her own in a strange place, surrounded by the one smell her mother had warned her to stay away from. She felt like turning over and falling back to sleep, but after a minute or two, her stomach once more alerted her to its increasingly empty nature. Time to go find some more of those delectable food cans that the humans put out so conveniently.

It didn't take long to fill her stomach once again, this time without any interruption. Apparently, the best time to scavenge for food was at night when humans were safely behind their closed and locked doors. Safe for them, and more importantly, she was safe from them as well. So, now what? She was now well rested and well fed. It must be time to go exploring. Maybe she'd be lucky and find she wasn't as far away from home as she'd originally thought. Maybe all those strange smells were masking her ability to detect the smells of her home.

As she left the safety of the pine trees, she remembered another lesson from her mother. They'd come upon a trail with a very hard surface where her mother stopped and lifted her nose in the air, but she'd been woolgathering and hadn't paid much attention, continuing to walk across to the other side. Suddenly, out of nowhere, a huge object moving at an incredible speed was upon her, followed a second later by a blast of noise that threatened to burst her eardrums. She leaped back just in time to avoid being smashed into roadkill. She turned to her mom for comfort, but instead received a thrashing, the likes of which she'd never experienced from her. The lesson was obvious. Such trails were dangerous and best avoided, which she did now.

Instead, she strolled along the side of the road, keeping a good six feet between her and the pavement until she no longer had a choice because there wasn't anything but pavement as she entered into Foster Flat proper. Strolling down the street, she was surrounded by an assortment of smells, many of which she didn't recognize. Then suddenly, up ahead she saw a form that set her heart to racing—a large black bear standing on all fours staring back at her. Could it be her mother? It certainly was the right size. As she took a few steps forward, she sniffed the air again but couldn't detect anything like her mother, nor anything like a bear. *Maybe the wind is blowing in the wrong direction*, she thought, but then realized there really wasn't even the slightest of breezes. The buildings seemed to be blocking it.

She continued to walk cautiously towards the bear when she noticed, several yards farther up the road, another form, this one a bear standing on its hind legs. As she approached the first bear, she stopped to sniff at it, but still, even this close, couldn't detect any familiar scent. Growing more confused by the minute, the bear cub strolled on to the second bear, circling around it, ready to jump out of the way if it tried to attack her, but she needn't have worried. Both bears seemed frozen in place. She came within a few inches of the second bear's hind legs and sniffed again. Still nothing. That's when she spied a third form farther up the road. This bear was sitting on its haunches with a second smaller bear about her own size sitting in front of the larger bear. A mother and her cub, just like her and her mother. Surely they could help her.

She trotted towards them, continuing to sniff the air as she went. Though she still couldn't detect any bear smells, she did begin to pick up the subtle odors that reminded her of her home. As she drew near, she noticed several sprigs of dry grass and a small pile of leaves upon which the two bears rested. The smells of home made his heart ache even more for her mother. At the same time, it was nice to find this tiny fragment of home in this strange land. She curled up next to the still bear cub and fell asleep.

AS MIMI RAWLINGS PARKED her bike in the bike stand and reached into its basket to retrieve her bagged lunch, she noticed a late model automobile driving down Main Street and pulling into one of the thirty-minute parking places just a few doors down from her mom's gift shop. She glanced down the street a little farther to the large town clock. Not even 8 AM yet. *Seems like the tourists start showing up earlier every year*, Mimi thought, shaking her head. *Don't they know that nothing opens for another hour? Well, except The Apothecary a couple blocks away that opens for breakfast at 6 AM.* It was one of the few things she liked about helping her mom open Narnia, the gift shop where her mother spent so much of her time. Mimi enjoyed the quiet mornings before the surge of out-of-towners descended on her town. She realized how essential the tourists were to the success of her mother's business, but that didn't mean she had to like them.

Mimi finished locking her bike to the stand and started walking towards her mother's store when she noticed the new additions to the street and her heart soared. The new Bearfooting Bears had been placed along Main Street since the last time she'd been downtown. These sculptured bears had become an annual event and a major fundraiser for several of the nonprofit organizations in the area, but what Mimi enjoyed most about them was the creativity exhibited by the local artists who decorated them, often using resources from the area.

Before entering Narnia, Mimi paused long enough to watch a small girl, probably no more than four or five years old, dressed in a bright pink pinafore dress, exit from the fancy auto and rushed over to the closest sculpture, a mother bear and her cub, her arms outstretched preparing to hug one of the bears. *Oh, how cute*, Mimi thought as she watched, remembering fondly her own first times with the bears during her preschool days. Despite having grown into a skeptical teenager, when it came to the Bearfooting Bears, she retained that childlike innocence that this small girl was now demonstrating.

Mimi started to turn to enter the store when a sudden movement caught her eye. Had that been the small cub that had moved? Surely they hadn't ruined the Bearfooting Bears by automating them, had they? Just as quickly as she had the thought, Mimi realized there were two small cubs, one that continued to lean against its mother and a second one that was very much alive and scurrying away from the little girl. The girl's mother let out a bloodcurdling scream that sent a chill up Mimi's back, but that her little girl ignored as she chased after the frightened cub.

"Missy Ann, you stay away from that dirty animal," the mother shouted. She looked around frantically for help. Spying Mimi looking on, she shouted. "Is that your filthy animal attacking my daughter?"

Is she talking to me? Mimi wondered. Her next thought was to straighten the woman out. *The animal isn't all that dirty, it's certainly not mine, and it looks to me like it's your daughter doing the attacking.* She opened her mouth to reply, but then closed it again, remembering her mother's warning earlier in the week: "Not every smart-aleck remark that comes to mind needs to be spoken."

Instead, she answered, "No ma'am, my mother won't let me keep a bear cub for a pet. Would you?"

The woman ignored her comment, turning back to her daughter. "Missy Ann! Come to me this instant," she shouted, with enough vinegar in her voice that even Mimi was tempted to comply. Missy Ann stopped in her tracks and watched as the bear cub rounded a corner and disappeared down a side alley.

"What kind of town is this that would allow a wild animal to threaten my poor little girl? Your mayor will hear about this." This last remark was directed to Mimi, who simply shrugged. She was more concerned with the baby bear than either the woman or her daughter. Ignoring the two tourists, Mimi ran to the alley to see if she could see the cub, but by the time she arrived, it was nowhere to be seen.

MAGINA MARTIN, CHAIRPERSON of the town council, banged on the desk in front of her for the third time. "Please, everyone sit down and shut up. Mayor Etheridge has the floor." She emphasized her demand with three more forceful raps with the gavel and a stern look that threatened to peel the paint off the meeting room walls.

"Thank you, Madame chairperson," the mayor replied, remaining standing as the other people around him finally sat down. "As I was saying, as the person representing the fine merchants of Foster Flat, we must take today's report of a wild animal on our Main Street seriously. That's why I called this emergency meeting and invited Bo Rawlings here along with his niece Mimi. As I'm sure you all know, Bo is one of our most respected citizens and an avid hunter and sportsman. Mimi is one of the only people who live in this area who has actually seen the beast." He waved his hand in the direction of the two Rawlings, then waved Bo back into his seat before he had a chance to finish standing up. "I'll have both of them speak in just a moment, but first, let me share with you just a few of my thoughts about this matter." Mayor Etheridge ignored the groans that came from several of the other citizens in attendance.

"As you all know, we're heading into a most important time of the year for Foster Flat—tourist season. So much of the continued prosperity of our fine town depends on these next six months. The last thing we need is for the word to spread that it's not safe to walk the streets of Foster Flat. Why, such a rumor could be devastating to our economy. That's why I say we need to nip this matter in the bud...in the bud I say."

There was a growing mumbling of consent from this last comment, followed with several "hear, hear," and "that's right."

"And how do you propose we 'nip this in the bud,' Mayor?" Magina asked, the gavel raised once again in an effort to subdue the others.

"We hunt down the vicious beast. I shoot it before it has a chance to accost any more of our fine visitors," Etheridge proclaimed.

"What?!" Mimi shouted before she realized what she was saying. "That's ridiculous. It was just a small, frightened bear cub."

Magina's gavel crashed down with forceful authority. "You'll have your turn to speak, Miss Mimi, but you do not have the floor at the moment."

Bo Rawlings patted his niece's knee as he stood up. "Magina...Mayor, if I may?"

Magina glanced over to the mayor, who nodded his ascent.

"Yes, Bo. You have the floor."

"Mayor Etheridge has already shared his proposal with me prior to this emergency meeting, which is one of the reasons I agreed to attend. Y'all know me to be a pretty simple, straightforward kind of guy, so I'll give it to you straight. We may indeed need to resort to shooting this animal who's taken it upon itself to visit our streets..."

"You're not serious..." Mimi started, but stopped when her uncle placed his hand on her head and squeezed it not so gently.

"...But I think such actions are premature. I recommend we first do our best to capture the beast and return it to the wild where it belongs. After all, we have over twenty statues of bears lining our streets for the twelfth year in a row. What kind of public relations nightmare would occur if the word got out that we'd killed a small, innocent bear cub that has stumbled into our town?"

"Why, it would show that we take the safety of our citizens and visitors seriously," Marcus Warren stood up, ignoring Magina's stern look and the raising of her gavel. He was a large man, easily over six feet, who looked even more imposing in his outfit of camo, complete with military style boots. "Listen, I'm not the only one at this meeting who depends on the tourist trade this time of year. My Army Surplus and Gun Shop makes over two-thirds of its revenue in these next six months. Beergut and I will be happy to take it upon ourselves to hunt this varmint down and eliminate the threat," he said as he slapped the man sitting next to him on the back with enough force to make Beergut wince in pain and move his chair out of range.

At this remark, Mimi's hand flew into the air, where she waved it back and forth. The chairperson's gaze flitted to her and then away, so Mimi added her second arm as she bounced in her seat. "Okay, let's move on," Magina said, continuing to ignore the teen. "Do we have a motion..."

"Excuse me, Madame Chairperson," Bo interrupted. "I believe you said that Mimi would have an opportunity to speak as well. She is the only one here that has actually seen the animal."

"Well..." Magina started, as she glanced at the Mayor again, who shrugged. "Okay, but just for a minute. We do have other business that needs our attention."

Bo nodded to his niece, who stood up, but then seemed frozen in place.

"Go on, Mimi," Bo encouraged her. "Say your piece."

Mimi nodded, took a deep breath, then let the words pour out. "Our recent visitor that y'all are so scared about is more afraid of us than we have any right to be afraid of her. She's a small bear cub, probably just a couple months old..."

"Yeah, but cubs grow up fast in these parts," Marcus interrupted, then shut up when Magina threatened him with her gavel.

"Sure they do, and that's why we need to do whatever we can to find him and get him back where he belongs," Mimi added. "As far back as I can remember, every year at this time, our little town has invested time, effort and money in our Bearfooting Fundraiser. In the process, we've become known as a 'bear-friendly' community." Mimi glanced around to see several people nodding in agreement. Bolstered by this, she continued. "Killing a small, innocent cub who's done nothing wrong other than stumble into our town and spend a night curled up next to the closest thing to a mother that he could find...well, it wouldn't be right, and it certainly isn't who we are. Least that's my view. Foster Flat is 'bear-friendly,' and we need to stay that way." With that, Mimi nodded to the chairperson that she was finished and sat down as several people in the audience applauded.

Magina pounded on the table in front of her again to silence the crowd. As she did so, Bo stood up. "Madame Chairperson, I'd like to make a motion that we do everything in our power over the next week to capture the cub. Since we don't know where it comes from, I further recommend we take it to the nature science center in Asheville once we apprehend it. I volunteer to head up this effort."

The motion was rapidly seconded and was passed by the council members unanimously.

AS EVERYONE FILED OUT of the meeting room, Mayor Etheridge motioned to Marcus to follow him out of the room and to his office adjacent to the council room.

"Come on, Beergut, let's go see what the mayor wants." The two men meandered among the crowd for a minute or two before quietly slipping into the mayor's office.

"You wanted to see us, Mr. Mayor?"

Etheridge looked up from where he was sitting behind his desk and frowned. "Actually, I wanted to see you...in private." He glared at Beergut, who simply stood there with a silly smile on his face.

"Sorry," Marcus replied. "I didn't..."

"Never mind," the mayor interrupted. "What I need to talk to you about will likely take more than just one man. Let him stay."

"What's on your mind?" Marcus asked.

"I take it from what you said in that meeting that you're no more happy about the outcome than I am."

Marcus nodded. "Seems like a waste of time to me. Plenty more bears where that one came from, but I don't know that there's much we can do about it. The vote passed unanimously."

Yeah, well, that's why you're not sitting in this seat, the mayor started to say, but then thought better of it.

"If there's one thing I've learned from my many years in politics, it's that sometimes leaders need to do what they know is right, and be damned what the public may think."

Marcus stared at him. "What are you saying?"

"Just that you seemed to have a viable plan of action as well. One that would resolve this matter once and for all. In fact, if it were handled properly, no one need be any the wiser about how the matter was resolved...if you get my drift."

Marcus glanced from the mayor to Beergut, who nodded. "Yeah, I get it. Is this an official request from the mayor's office?"

Etheridge paused for a moment before replying. "If you're discovered, the mayor's office will deny having any knowledge of the incident."

Marcus frowned.

"But I can tell you this. Walter Etheridge, private citizen and one of the wealthiest men in the county, never forgets a favor."

"That's good enough for me," Marcus replied. "Let's go, Beergut. We've got work to do."

MIMI SAT WITH HER BACK to the Oriental maple, which did a good job of hiding her from view, and checked her supplies for the third time: binoculars that allowed her to see clearly down most of Main Street, sleeping bag just in case it turned into a long night or grew too cool in the early morning hours, four ham and cheese sandwiches (down from the original six she'd brought), and a quart bottle of Fresca, still half full even after she'd used it to wash down the other two sandwiches. She sure hoped her little bear cub friend liked ham and cheese as much as she did. She slid to one side and reached beneath her rump to pull out the collar and leash that she hoped to slip on the bear cub if or when he showed up.

Everything is ready, she thought as she twisted around to take another look at the large clock hanging over the Foster Flat Mineral and Lapidary Museum. Eleven-seventeen and the main thoroughfare is closed up tighter than a tick on a hound. That's what she loved about the town where she'd grown up. No late night shenanigans for her town. Well, except possibly tonight if she was lucky. Straightening up, she picked up the binoculars and studied the street for any sign of a small black bear cub.

"Please show up," she muttered to herself. "I really don't want to sit out here all night long. I brought you some ham and cheese sandwiches. My mom makes the best sandwiches around. She really does." She thought about eating another one herself, but then thought better of it. Those sandwiches need to last the night as well as being an enticement to the bear that had her out here in the first place.

Time paced slowly in the quiet little town and after a full day of school, followed by helping her mom at the store, it wasn't long before Mimi found herself dozing off. She'd pulled the sleeping bag up over her legs and abdomen to stave off the dropping temperature, but the cozy little nest she'd made for herself just made it that much harder to stay awake. Luckily the old clock chimed every fifteen minutes and marked the hour with deep bongs for each hour passed, so she could catch little catnaps without being concerned she'd spend the night sound asleep and miss the bear.

MEANWHILE, THE BEAR cub had taken refuge in a small park a block off of Main Street, staying hidden most of the time from the few humans that passed through its walkways. She'd already checked out the two garbage cans at either end of the park, but came up with nothing more than the remains of a sausage and egg biscuit, which she had readily consumed several hours ago. She'd then crawled back under the bushes, where she'd spent the rest of the day and much of the evening until, once again, the need to relieve her hunger and thirst grew more important than staying safely hidden.

She recalled seeing a large dumpster in the alleyway she had run down that morning to escape from the angry human with the screechy voice. She returned to it now but was disappointed to find that the dumpster's contents were securely locked away despite all her efforts. Frustrated, she walked slowly to the other end of the alley in the direction of Main Street, sniffing the night air.

What was that delectable smell coming from that direction? There were a number of interesting smells, many of which she didn't recognize, but one particular one had to be food. It just smelled too good not to be edible. Besides, there were also the familiar odors of her old home she'd detected the night before. That combination was simply too much to ignore. She eased herself out onto Main Street.

"DO YOU SEE HER? WHAT'S she doing now?" Beergut asked, trying unsuccessfully to take the binoculars from Marcus, who pushed his hands away. The two men stood on the second floor of Marcus's Army Surplus store that gave them a full view of Main Street as far north as the Mast General Store.

"She's doing the same thing she was doing ten minutes ago when you asked. Nothing. Not a damn-blasted thing." He lowered the binoculars and reached in the back pocket of his fatigues for the flask. He took a long draught of the liquid before reluctantly surrendering it to his partner.

"Not too much," he warned. "We need to stay alert."

"Sure thing, Boss," Beergut replied, then took an equally long pull on the mouth of the flask. "Warms all the way down, it does."

"What if the bear don't show?" Beergut asked, reluctantly returning the flask to its owner.

"Then we return here tomorrow night and the night after that," Marcus replied with a disgusted sneer on his face.

"Seems like a lot of fuss over a little ol' bear," Beergut said, "especially considering we're not getting paid."

"I wouldn't be so sure about that."

"What do you mean?" Beergut asked.

"Well, besides our corrupt mayor owing us a big favor, I took the liberty of making a call today to an old Army buddy of mine down in Atlanta. He's got a pretty sweet deal going...illegal as hell, but just that much sweeter because of the stupid laws."

"What's that?"

"He sells wild animals," Marcus said, as he raised the binoculars to his eyes again and leaned out the window to get a better view north and south. "He told me if we brought him a black bear cub alive and in relatively good shape, he'd pay us $500 for it."

"You're shitting me," Beergut replied, a skeptical look on his face.

"Honest to god truth. Damn thing will be out of our hair and we'll make a few hundred bucks to boot. Hell, we play our cards right, we won't even have to catch it. We'll let little ol' Mimi do the work for us."

There she is! Mimi sat up straight, her heart beating rapidly at the sight of the bear cub sniffing around the same statue of the mama bear and her cub where she'd seen her the night before. *I wonder what's so special about that particular pair,* she thought as she reached into the paper bag to pull out one of the ham and cheese sandwiches. *Well, here goes nothing.* She slowly crawled from her hiding place, sandwich in one hand, leash and collar in the other. The baby bear continued to sniff around the statue so intently that Mimi was able to get within ten feet before the cub looked up.

Mimi held out the sandwich and whispered in a soothing voice. "I brought this for you. It's ham and cheese, and you can take my word for it, it's delicious." She gently waved it in the bear's direction and watched as the cub raised its nose to take a whiff. Mimi broke off one corner of the sandwich, making sure it had a piece of ham and cheese between the toasted slices of bread and tossed it in the cub's direction. It landed a foot or two away from her. After a moment of hesitation, the cub walked over to it, sniffed at it, and then quickly gulped it down.

"Didn't I tell you it was good?" Mimi said, chuckling softly at the satisfied look on the baby bear's face. *It's so cute*, she thought, then stopped herself. She studied the bear more closely, finally deciding the cub must be a female. *At least until someone like my uncle tells me otherwise,* she thought. She broke off another corner of the sandwich and tossed it a couple feet from the bear, bending down as she did so. With much less hesitation this time, the bear walked over to the morsel of food and downed it quickly before looking up at the remaining sandwich in Mimi's hand.

"You want the rest of this?" Mimi asked, as she placed the sandwich down next to her. "Come and get it. I promise I won't hurt you."

She watched as the bear eyed first the sandwich and then her. "There's more where that came from as well. As many sandwiches as you can eat," Mimi assured her. "I've even got one with extra mayo if you like, but let's start with this one." She reached out and slid the sandwich a few inches closer to the bear, who took a couple long sniffs before stepping cautiously forward. Mimi pretended not to pay any attention, but watched out of the corner of her eye as the cub slowly creep forward. When it finally reached the sandwich and started eating it, Mimi reached out and slowly placed the collar around the cub's neck while whispering to her gently. "It's going to be all right. We're going to get you home somehow." *But where was that?* As she asked herself that question, she glanced up to the statue of the mama bear and her cub, and suddenly knew the answer. She smiled as she watched the cub finish off the sandwich and look around for more.

"Still hungry, huh? Well, I've got more right over there," she said, pointing behind her. "Let's just walk over and see if I can't find the one with the extra may…"

"That won't be necessary," a rough voice interrupted. As Mimi turned around, she felt a calloused hand grab her arm and wrench the leash away. *Marcus and Beergut! Where the hell did they come from?*

"We'll take it from here," Marcus continued, as he handed the leash to his partner, with the now frightened bear at the other end fighting against the constraint of the leash and collar. "Take the scruffy thing to the truck and stuff it in the cage that's in the back."

"Leave her alone!" Mimi shouted, starting towards Beergut, but Marcus stepped in to block her way.

"Now you know better than to give us any trouble." He pushed her roughly away. "Stand aside. We are on official town business."

"Like hell you are," Mimi retorted, trying to push him back, but since Marcus outweighed her by over a hundred pounds, he only laughed.

"Look, girlie, I really don't want to hurt you, but if you get in my way, I'll have no choice. " He shoved her again, this time much harder. Mimi stumbled backward, falling to the ground, her head hitting something hard and unforgiving. She saw stars and felt like she was going to pass out. Then she heard the first rumblings of a growl.

"What was that?" Beergut asked. "Did you hear it?"

Marcus looked around, suddenly wary. "It was nothing. Just some heat lightning," he replied in an unconvincing tone. He turned his attention back to Beergut. "I thought I told you to take the little shit to the truck." But before either of them could move, they heard a second growl, this one much louder and appearing to come from several different directions.

"Holy Mother of..." Beergut shouted. "What the hell is going on? Did you see that?" He pointed down the street at one of the other bear figures about a half block away. This one stood on its hind legs with its front paws in the air. "That damn bear just moved!"

"Don't be ridiculous," Marcus shouted back. "It's a damn stat...What the...?"

Mimi sat up on one elbow and felt the back of her head where a lump was already forming. She stared down the street where Beergut had pointed, but she couldn't get her eyes to focus properly. Even so, it appeared that the bear in question no longer possessed the shiny veneer of its former self, and it was advancing on them on legs that appeared quite mobile.

Suddenly, a third and then a fourth growl cut through the night air as other bears came to life, obviously upset by the antics they'd been witnessing, and advanced towards the two men. Beergut dropped the end of the leash and the bear cub scampered away from him and towards Mimi, who had managed to push herself to a sitting position on the sidewalk. She reached out her arms and the cub came to her.

"This can't be happening," Marcus exclaimed, though the look of terror on his face confirmed he didn't believe his own statement. The two men stood back to back while they slowly retreated in the direction of Marcus's truck, as several of the Bearfooting bears herded them in that direction, growling their dislike for the men.

"I told you Foster Flat was a bear-friendly town," Mimi yelled after them. "I just had no idea how bear-friendly," she muttered more softly. "No idea at all." She suddenly felt very sleepy and her head hurt something awful. "I think I better lie down for just a minute," she whispered softly to the bear cub, who nuzzled against her.

MIMI TRIED TO SLAP the hand on her shoulder away. "Please, Mom, just a few more minutes," she muttered. "I don't want any breakfast this morning."

But the hand continued to shake her. "Wake up, Mimi," a gruff voice, clearly not her mother's, said.

She opened her eyes to see her Uncle Bo towering over her, a concerned look on his face. "I thought you were going to call me when the bear cub showed up," he said.

"I was...I will...I," Mimi tried to answer, but was still too groggy to make any sense. She tried again. "I was going to call but then it got kinda crazy, and I guess I forgot." She raised one hand to the back of her head and felt the lump. No wonder her head was hurting so much. It all started coming back to her: the bear cub's appearance, followed by Marcus and Beergut trying to take the cub from her, and then...nah, that couldn't have happened, could it?

"Well, no matter, I see you've made friends with the little guy," Bo replied.

"Gal," Mimi corrected, as she slowly sat up and felt the world spin around her for a moment. She looked over to see the bear cub lying quietly next to the Bearfooting statue. "I'm pretty sure she's a she," Mimi continued.

Bo took a closer look at the cub as it started to move around. "You may be right. It can be pretty hard to tell when they're young."

Mimi reached up with her left hand to brush the hair from her face and noticed for the first time the leash still wrapped around her hand.

"We'll take her home for now, and I'll drop her off at the nature center tomorrow," Bo said as he started to reach for the leash.

"No!' Mimi shouted, jerking the leash out of his reach.

"What? That was the plan we agreed to with the town council."

"That was before we knew where she came from," Mimi countered. She rose slowly, then waited for the world to stop spinning before straightening up.

"But we don't know where she's from...do we?" Bo asked, a perplexed look growing on his face.

Mimi pointed to the statue. "I think she's drawn to that statue because parts of it came from her home area." She pointed to the writing on the back of the statue. "It says here that this one was decorated by the Blue Ridge Rafting Company. They're a whitewater rafting business located in the Nantahala valley area. I bet if we go there we'll find her mother."

"But that's over thirty miles from here. How could she..."

"I don't know," Mimi interrupted him, "but I have a strong hunch that's where she's from. We've got to at least give it a try."

Bo nodded slowly. "Okay, I guess we can give it a shot." He glanced at his watch. "It'll be sunrise soon. We can head in that direction, but if we don't find her mother..."

"Then we'll decide the next step," Mimi finished for him.

"I put Lucy's dog pen in the back of the truck yesterday."

"That's okay," Mimi said as she started walking towards her uncle's truck, the cub following behind her. "She can sit in the cab with us."

Bo shook his head. "I swear you're getting as bossy as your mother."

"It runs in the family," Mimi retorted.

THE FIRST THINGS MIMI noticed as Bo pulled into the Nantahala River camp and canoe park were two signs. The first was a simple sign tacked to a post: *Bear Sanctuary*. The second was a life-size replica of Yogi Bear holding its own sign: *Hi Kids! Don't feed the bears. Be sure Dad keeps the car windows rolled up*, and in much smaller type, *Over 40 people have been hurt by bears this year*.

Cute sign, Mimi thought, as she patted the bear cub's head, *with a serious message*.

"I think we're in the right place," she said, as Bo stopped the truck and put it in park.

"Could be," Bo replied, "but I wouldn't get your hopes up just yet. This is part of the Nantahala National Forest, which spans over 500,000 acres. In other words, there's a lot of land where his mother could be."

"Her," Mimi corrected him again. "That's okay. I have a good feeling about this place."

"Well, it's sure off the beaten track enough," Bo replied. "If my truck didn't have four-wheel drive, I'm not sure we would have made it back here."

As Mimi climbed out of the truck, she looked around, verifying what she already suspected. They were all alone, though there were some tire tracks that appeared to be fairly recent. "Come on, Gallie, let's go find your mama," she said, as she pulled gently on the leash.

"Gallie?"

"Yep, that's her name."

"Don't tell me you've named her. You know better than to do that. You name an animal, then you start getting attached..."

"I know, I know." Mimi stopped him. "You've told me that a dozen times, but I'm already attached. I also know that Gallie needs to be out here with her mother, so quit worrying and help me find her."

"And how do you suggest we do that?"

Mimi considered the question, but came up blank.

"I'm not sure. I hadn't gotten that far in my thinking."

Bo groaned. Then, looking around, he pointed off in the distance. "Looks like there's a clearing about halfway up that mountain. Let's see if we can find a trail and take a hike. Who knows, we might get lucky." He pulled a couple bottles of water out of the truck cab and tossed one to his niece.

Mimi caught the bottle, nodded, and together they headed in the direction Bo had pointed. Sure enough, at the edge of the parking area, they found a well-worn path. The three of them trekked for close to an hour before they finally reached the clearing, which turned out to be a large growth of blueberry bushes.

"It's not quite the time for blueberries to be ripe yet, but I figured this would be a likely place for a mama bear to hang out," Bo said as he picked a few of the unripened berries from a nearby bush.

"Now what?"

"You tell me. This was your idea, remember."

Mimi frowned. This was beginning to feel like a bad idea after all.

"Why don't you let him...I mean her...off the leash and see what happens," Bo said, more gently.

"What if she runs off?" Mimi asked.

Bo shrugged. "She seems pretty taken with you. I don't think she'll go far."

Mimi nodded. *Hell, I don't have any better plan*, she thought. *I may as well give it a try.*

She pulled Gallie to her and removed the collar. At first, the bear cub just stood there and looked up at her. "Go on. Go find your mother," Mimi urged her, then pushed her gently with one foot.

Finally, realizing she was free, she turned and trotted away several feet before stopping. She rose on her back haunches and sniffed the air before letting out a sound that sounded to Mimi remarkably like a baby crying for its mother. Gallie repeated it several times, took a few more steps forward, then repeated the cry.

The sound wrenched at Mimi's heart. *Oh baby, my poor baby,* she thought. Gallie strolled to the edge of the clearing and called again, but again she was met only with silence. Finally, she lay down with her face between her paws.

Bo and Mimi looked on and waited. Finally, Bo said, "Well, it was worth a try. Why don't you put her collar back on and we'll..."

But the roar of a bear off in the distance stopped him in his tracks.

"What the...?" Mimi asked. "Was that her?"

Bo pointed to the bear cub, who was now standing on its hind legs and sniffing the air in the direction the sound had come from. Before he could answer Mimi, Gallie replied with her own roar, though it was several octaves higher and still sounded more like the cry of a human child. Several seconds later, they heard another roar, this time coming from much closer.

"Ahh, we need to not be here when that mama bear arrives," Bo said, as he reached out, took Mimi's hand and started pulling her back towards the path.

"But I can't just leave her," Mimi replied as she dug in her heels. "What if that's not her mother?"

"Oh, that's her mother all right," Bo replied. He turned back to his niece and, looking her straight in the face, said, "You've helped her return to her home, Mimi. Now it's time for us to return to ours."

Mimi stared back. She knew her uncle was right. He'd never steered her wrong, especially when it came to matters of nature. She nodded, then turned back to the bear cub. "Bye-bye, Gallie girl. Have a great life." And with that, she allowed her uncle to lead her away.

The End

Check out these other books by Orrin Jason Bradford

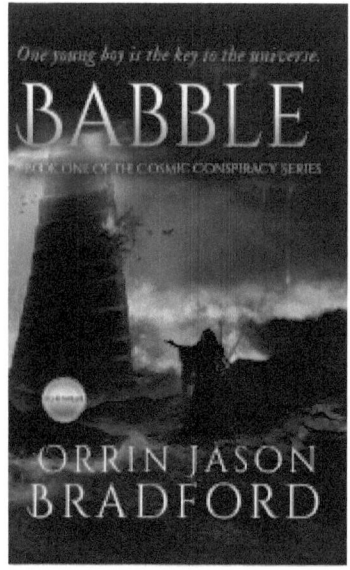

On the brink of a new age, the human race leaps forward into the evolutionary void and changes the course of human history forever. For young Bobbie Cagle, the normal difficulties of growing up are overshadowed by his unique condition. Bobbie's inability to communicate normally is misdiagnosed for years as autism, and masks the great part in history he is destined to play. His unique ability to create beautiful works of art is just the tip of the iceberg.
myBook.to/Babble

In a world full of stories, the usual and the unusual combine to reveal the beauty of the universe...
Celebrating the normal, and not so normal, of everyday life, *Hunt Along the Iron River and Other Timeless Tales* bears witness to the uniqueness of a singular experience, and the wonder of the universe.
myBook.to/HuntAnthology

A Message from Orrin Jason Bradford (aka W. Bradford Swift)

As an Indie Author I know just how important readers are. Without people who enjoy reading, authors are pretty useless. Oh, I know I enjoy the thrill of writing the *next great American novel,* but that's really not enough. I need readers like you who enjoy reading my stories. So, thank you. I sincerely appreciate your taking the time to read this second volume of *Fantastic Fables of Foster Flat.*

Perhaps you would enjoy some of my other books and stories. If you'd like to stay up to date on new book releases, special discounts, and my occasional giveaways, you can also join my **OJB's Amazingly Awesome Readers Group**. Just go to my author's website and blog where you can also download a free copy of one of my other books:www.wbradfordswift.com. There's one last thing you could do if you be so king. Go to your favorite onine bookstore and leave an honest review of *Fantastic Fables of Foster Flat.* Honest reviews are really important to help other readers like you know which books to try next. And thanks for being an amazingly awesome reader.

Orrin Jason Bradford (aka W. Bradford Swift)

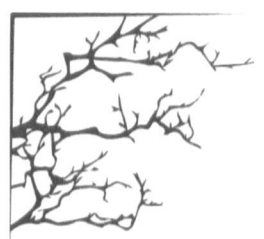

About the Author

Orrin Jason Bradford is the pen name W. Bradford Swift uses for his adult fiction to distinguish it from his nonfiction and young adult novels. An avid reader from childhood, he continues to read and study science fiction and fantasy. As a young man he promised one day to write his own fiction in gratitude to the many authors who kept him entertained and more or less sane over the years.

Swift is best known for his visionary fiction and nonfiction that "entertain while also enlightening and encouraging the reader to expand their sense of what is possible, and then applying that expanded awareness to their life." He is a graduate of Clarion West in Seattle, WA – a residential workshop for writers of science fiction and fantasy. He lives in the "paradise found" of the Blue Ridge Mountains of North Carolina with his wife, Ann, their daughter, Amber and a menagerie of four-legged family members.

His other speculative fiction includes the six-book *FreeForm* science fiction thriller series, *Babble,* and *Stars Beckon Call.* He is also the author of visionary nonfiction including: *Life On Purpose: Six Passages to an Inspired Life, Spiral of Fulfillment: Living an Inspired Life of Service, Simplicity and Spiritual Serenity,* and *From Spark to Flame: Fanning Your Passion & Ideas into Money-making Magazine Articles that Make a Difference.* To learn more about additional stories and books by the author go to: www.wbradfordswift.com[1]

---

1. http://www.wbradfordswift.com/

Porpoise Publishing
Flat Rock, NC 28731
www.lifeonpurpose.com
Library of Congress Cataloging-in-Publication Data
Fantastic Fables of Foster Flat (Volume 2)/ W. Bradford Swift
ISBN-13: 978-1930328761 (Physical Book)
1. Fantasy anthology 2. Speculative Fiction 3. Tales with a Twist

Cover design by Victor Habbick
Typeset in Book Palatino
Printed in USA
First Edition

About the Publisher

Porpoise Publishing is the imprint of indie author W. Bradford Swift who also writes under the pen name of Orrin Jason Bradford. It is best known for publishing visionary fiction--stories that entertain while also inspiring readers to imagine greater possibilities for their lives.

www.ingramcontent.com/pod-product-compliance
Lightning Source LLC
Chambersburg PA
CBHW020731210626
46807CB00016B/1487